Acclaim *for* the authors of
SUMMER DREAMS

STEVI MITTMAN

"Humor, excitement, a good mystery and romantic uncertainty make this series a winner."
Top Pick! 4½ stars
> —*Romantic Times BOOKreviews* on
> *What Goes with Blood Red, Anyway?*

"Don't miss this book—it has all the heart her historicals held, as well as Stevi's wonderful and wacky sense of humor."
> —*USA TODAY* bestselling author Elizabeth Boyle
> on *Who Makes Up These Rules, Anyway?*

KATE AUSTIN

"A lively modern story of change, hope and fulfillment."
> —*Library Journal* on *The Sunshine Coast News*

"Filled with vividly felt emotion, a love of reading, unexpected turns and wonderful, fresh characters, this is a book readers won't be able to put down."
> —*Romantic Times BOOKreviews* on
> *Awakening*

JENNIFER GREENE

"A book by Jennifer Greene hums with an unbeatable combination of sexual chemistry and heartwarming emotion."
> —*New York Times* bestselling author
> Susan Elizabeth Phillips

"A spellbinding storyteller of uncommon brilliance, the fabulous Jennifer Greene is one of the romance genre's greatest gifts to the world of popular fiction."
> —*Romantic Times BOOKreviews*

Stevi Mittman has always been a decorator at heart. The Teddi Bayer murder mysteries have allowed her to combine her love of writing and her passion for decorating, and she couldn't be happier. As a fictional decorator she doles out advice on Teddi's Web site, TipsFromTeddi.com, and receives and responds to e-mails on behalf of Teddi.

Decorating is a third career for the prolific Mittman, who is also a stained-glass artist with work in the Museum of the City of New York and private commissions around the country and, of course, an award-winning author. Visit her at www.stevimittman.com.

Kate Austin has worked as a legal assistant, a commercial fisher, a brewery manager, a teacher, a technical writer and a herring popper, while managing to read an average of a book a day. Go ahead—ask her anything. If she doesn't know the answer she'll make it up, because she's been reading and writing fiction for as long as she can remember.

She blames her mother and her two grandmothers for her reading and writing obsession. She lives in Vancouver, Canada, where she can walk on the beach whenever necessary, even in the rain.

She'd be delighted to hear from readers through her Web site, www.kateaustin.ca.

Jennifer Greene lives near Lake Michigan with her husband and two children. Before writing full-time, she worked as a teacher and a personnel manager. Michigan State University honored her as an "outstanding woman graduate" for her work with women on campus.

Ms. Greene has written more than fifty category romances, for which she has won numerous awards, including two RITA® Awards from the Romance Writers of America in the Best Short Contemporary Books category, and a Career Achievement Award from *Romantic Times BOOKreviews* magazine.

THE Nxt NOVEL™

Summer Dreams

Stevi Mittman

Kate Austin

Jennifer Greene

SUMMER DREAMS

copyright © 2007 by Harlequin Books S.A.

isbn-13:978-0-373-88138-3

isbn-10:   0-373-88138-X

The publisher acknowledges the copyright holders of the individual
works as follows:

WHO'S THAT IN THE ITSY-BITSY, ANYWAY?
copyright © 2007 by Stephanie Mittman

SUMMERTIME BLUES
copyright © 2007 by Kate Austin

KOKOMO
copyright © 2007 by Alison Hart

TheNextNovel.com

 HARLEQUIN®

PRINTED IN U.S.A.

CONTENTS

WHO'S THAT IN THE ITSY-BITSY, ANYWAY?

STEVI MITTMAN

From the Author

Dear Reader,

I love summer. I'd love it more if I looked better in a bathing suit, but if it means long lazy days, warm nights and trips in the convertible to the ice cream stand, then I'll deal.

I love family. Love those loud, crazy, chaotic gatherings where shouting is not about anger, but rather a desire to be heard.

I love romance. I've been in love with the same man since I was in high school, and the love just gets better and deeper and freer the older we get.

I love a puzzle. How does it go together? How do all the pieces fit?

I love laughter. Of all the noises in the universe, is there a better, more contagious sound?

I hope I've given you all the things I love in "Who's That in the Itsy Bitsy, Anyway?" because in addition to summer, family, romance, puzzles and laughter, I love you, dear reader! You give meaning to the days I spend with my laptop under a beach umbrella on the deck or by a cozy fire in the living room.

Thanks for reading!

Love,

Stevi

This book is dedicated to DP, who started
the whole story years ago when he renovated his garage.

And to the usual suspects—you know who you are.

Thanks, as always, for cheering me on, laughing at the
right spots and reminding me it isn't brain surgery.

Love you!

CHAPTER 1

Late May

"Are you out of your mind?" my friend and partner in our decorating business, Bobbie Lyons, asks me as we come in from the heat and I plop down on the stool in her kitchen. Considering the fact that I've just told her that Carmine De'Guiseppe has offered to foot the bill for four weeks at sleepaway camp for all three of my children so that I can move into his house in the Hamptons and renovate it, her reaction isn't exactly surprising.

She reaches into her fridge and hands me a nice cold can of diet soda which I hold against my throat. "Because I'm considering doing it? Or because I haven't accepted it?"

I know, I know. It sounds like a slam dunk. But it's more complicated than it sounds. For starters, there's the fact that Carmine was, once upon a time, my mother's boyfriend. I mean, way, way back when dinosaurs roamed the earth, and before DNA testing could prove paternity, if you get my drift.

And then, it's a well-known fact that the man has definite Mafia connections. I'm not exactly sure what they are, but I am sure I don't want to get involved with anything even remotely involving the Mafia—not after finally extricating myself from my ex-husband and his friends with body parts for middle names.

One *Nicky the Nose* was enough for my lifetime, thank you very much.

Bobbie, hair in place, makeup perfect despite the heat, tips down the sunglasses she hasn't yet taken off, and studies me over the rims. She gives me one of her *let me get this straight* looks, which is just this side of her *please tell me you're kidding* looks. "Four weeks in the Hamptons without the kids? Teddi, I'd be there in a heartbeat if Mike and I weren't going on that cruise to Alaska."

In the imaginary *Go For It* column, I put as Number One the fact that Bobbie's twin girls will be off at camp, leaving my eldest, Dana, bored out of her skull. Number Two: Bobbie and Mike won't be around to help even up the parent-to-child ratio with all three of mine. And Number Three: How about the fact that it's only May and today it hit ninety-one degrees and I don't have central air-conditioning?

Then, in the *No How, No Way* column, I chalk in my mother's name. No, make that *chisel* in. She's permanently in that column, but this time it's worse than usual because the woman is way too interested in Carmine lately, and not nearly interested enough in Number Two on my *No How, No Way* list—my father. I just can't imagine telling him that I'm going to decorate Carmine's house while the man sends my father's grandchildren to camp.

When I tell Bobbie as much, she shrugs and asks why I'm so obsessed with "full disclosure."

"Well," I remind her, "unlike your mother, mine doesn't live three thousand miles away. She doesn't have your mother's philosophy of 'live and let live,' either. You know as well as I do that her nose job wasn't just to make her look better, but to help her sniff out every last detail of my life, the better to interfere in it."

Bobbie, who doesn't have to worry about calories, puts some chips in a bowl on the counter in front of me while I continue.

"That little turned up hook at the end of her nose that makes you think of Candice Bergen? A direct result of sticking it in everyone else's business."

Bobbie examines a chip as though there is a hidden message embedded within it. "Yeah, yeah," she says, because she's heard it all before. "So just don't tell her."

Like it's as simple as that and Swami June won't somehow divine the truth.

"Come on," Bobbie tells me. "You're smart. Get her to send you off with a smile."

"A smile? With all that Botox, I can't even tell if she's smiling. Besides, the only thing that could make her happy is if I tell her I'm going out to the Hamptons to marry a plastic surgeon."

There's a beat, and then Bobbie and I grin slowly at each other.

"Maybe not *marrying*," Bobbie says. "But what about *fishing* in the Hamptons. After all, what better place to catch a sturgeon? Or did you say surgeon?"

Four weeks in the Hamptons. Without the kids. I imagine Detective Drew Scoones and me on chaise lounges with cold drinks in our hands, ocean waves crashing in the background.

Drew and I recreating that scene in *From Here to Eternity*. Drew and I going inside.

"Mark could take care of Maggie May, I bet," Bobbie says. Maggie May? Oh, right. I forgot I even have a dog. "He loves to do little favors for you."

That's Bobbie—dig, dig, dig. I ignore her and tell her that Carmine says it's in terrible shape. His sister furnished it and used it for a couple of summers in the late fifties, but no one's been in it in years. I am trying desperately to keep a lid on my excitement because that's what I do—I prepare myself for disappointment.

Bobbie nods. "You're right," she says, smiling slyly. "You really shouldn't go. I mean, when you could just stay home and entertain three whiny kids…without my help…hey, you could get lucky. The ice cream man might come around! That'd be exciting."

Only, I admit, if he was in his early forties and drop-dead gorgeous.

But it's the thought of Alyssa sticking to my thighs when she sits on my lap, the idea of Jesse sitting in a dark room playing video games all day, the image of Dana hanging out with the boys at the community pool in a bathing suit that shows she's not a little girl anymore, that pushes me over the edge.

Okay, fine. So it's also that *Here to Eternity* thing. I may be nearly forty, but I'm not dead.

I pick up Bobbie's phone and dial my mother. Her caller ID tells her that it's Bobbie, so her first words are, "What's happened to Teddi now?"

I identify myself, have to go through hoops about why I'm calling from Bobbie's phone, and by the time I get to my news, she's totally exhausted me. "I'm calling for your advice," I say, and Bobbie nods emphatically, approving of my approach. "I have a chance to do a small house in the Hamptons in July, and I think I can swing sending the kids away to camp with some of the deposit, but I'm just not sure…."

"The Hamptons in July is the only place to be," my mother tells me. "That is, if you're serious about ever getting married again, and this time to someone worthwhile."

"So you think there might be some men out there?" I ask innocently, while Bobbie does her *I have to pee but I don't want to miss this* dance. "Really?"

My mother tells me if I don't eat another thing until July, there's a chance I *might* look decent enough in a bathing suit. I don't point out that I have no intention of being buried in a bathing suit, and that if I don't eat…

She insists that I sit down and have a heart-to-heart with my friend Howard before I go, so that I'll be able to tell the gay men from the straight ones. "This is very important," she tells me. "I mean, you aren't going to Fire Island, thank God, but still…We can't have you wasting your time like you did with Howard."

I don't point out that she was the one who thought that Howard was my soul mate, not to mention a great catch. And, technically she was right. She was just a little "disoriented." He was a great catch not for me, but for Nick Watts. And as soon as Nick's divorce from Madison, the Demon Barber of Park Avenue, comes through, they'll be heading up to Vermont to get married—the better to raise Nick and Madison's daughter. (Did I mention Madison's in prison for killing the health inspector and trying to kill Howard and me?)

Perhaps another time, because right now the conversation with my mother is going great. She wants to look over what

I'm going to bring out there to wear, she wants to treat me to a haircut. I'm thinking I'm *home free*.

And then, when I'm least expecting it, she turns the knife.

"So what idiot is giving up being in the Hamptons in July just so you can redecorate?"

CHAPTER 2

Monday, June 28th

I've kissed my sweet children goodbye and put them on a bus headed for Camp Runamuk. I've kissed Bobbie and Mike goodbye and put them on a ship bound for Alaska. I've kissed Maggie May goodbye and put her in a carrier in Mark's pickup for her vacation at his place.

And I've kissed my hot house and my ordinary life goodbye and hit the road for the Hamptons.

So can anyone tell me why I am now sitting outside a darling cottage on the water feeling like *what have I done? Where are my babies? My friends? My stupid dog?*

It's a really cute little house on a quiet street that's not quite as tony as the ones around it. My guess is that all the houses on this block were built in the fifties as refuges from the hot city and their owners are just biding their time while the market soars. Eventually they will be bought out one by one by people who will raze their sweet cottages and build ugly mansions that stretch from property line to property line.

I get out of my car and I can hear the ocean lapping at the shore. The sky is so blue it hurts my eyes. There is an old white picket fence and an arbor which leads to the front door. Behind the fence, which is peeling and missing a few of its slats, a bit of sea grass fills what passes for a front lawn. The smell of the ocean is everywhere, and I inhale greedily.

Four weeks will not be enough. A lifetime wouldn't be enough in a place like this.

I pull the keys from my purse and open the front door, which resists me. As I look around me, my words echo in my head, mocking me. *Four weeks will not be enough.*

I can't say that Carmine didn't warn me. He said his sister had used discarded furniture from her house and that even he knew it wasn't in good taste. But now that he is interested in using the place again, he wants it to look like a really classy beach house, and not, as he put it, "like Archie Bunker's den."

I look around, not quite believing what I'm seeing. This wonderful cottage on the water, which should be full of white and wicker and brightness, is furnished in Early American. George Washington himself is dancing with Martha on the blue-and-cream-colored toile fabric on the couch, in front of which is a plastic coffee table with some dying flowers in a vase. There's one of those wagon wheel lamps over a maple trestle table with captain's chairs.

The carpet, unbelievably, is orange.

A lifetime won't be enough to fix up a place like this.

Worst of all, outside the back windows is a small patio which ends at a wall which totally blocks any view of the ocean. Carmine alluded to a falling-out with his sister that ended her use of the house, and I'm willing to guess what it was probably over. I'm not surprised she didn't come back. I'd never show my face again after doing this. That's for sure.

I pull out my cellphone and punch up Mark, who, besides being a great dog sitter, is also the contractor who works with me. "Bring something to knock down a wall," I tell him, "and find out if the Salvation Army has a statute of limitations on furniture."

I go from room to room opening the windows to let in the ocean breeze, surprised by how little dust there is in the house. In the bedroom, I find the bed neatly made. On the nightstand is a half-empty bottle of wine and a candle burned nearly to its end. I hold the wine bottle at arm's length as I carry it to the kitchen to pour it down the drain, expecting the rancid smell of vinegar.

But I smell only wine.

Hmm. Dying, but not dead, flowers. Unspoiled wine. I open the refrigerator—one of those fifties types with those wonderful latches that remind me of the old Good Humor trucks. Inside there are a few cans of Coke and a pizza carton with two slices of mushroom pizza still inside. Being a mother, I can tell the age of leftover pizza at a glance, and this hasn't been here more than twenty-four hours. My stomach rumbles and I consider taking one of the slices, but having watched Howard recover from food poisoning after Madison gave him poisoned mushrooms, I think I'll pass.

In the freezer (another latch, and those wonderful old aluminum ice cube trays that never did work well), is a container of Häagen-Dazs. I bet no one ever died from poisoned Häagen-Dazs. And it's coffee. My favorite flavor. (How do I know? Okay, I opened it and it's half gone. Happy now?)

I flip open my cell phone again and hit the speed dial for Drew Scoones. Drew is my…my… Okay, maybe it's better to start with what Drew is not. He's not my boyfriend. He's not my friend, at all. He's the cop who investigated the murder of my first client, and my mother's disappearance, and my erogenous zones. He was Johnny-on-the-spot when my mother discovered a dead body in the men's room, and when my G-spot went missing, he was the one to find it. He's the detective who lifts suspects' prints from crime scenes and leaves his own prints on my… Enough of that.

I call Drew. And when he answers, I say, "I think—like the three bears—someone's been sleeping in *my* bed."

"And enjoying every minute," he says without missing a beat.

I tell him that I don't mean him and tell him what I've found.

"Probably a couple of kids fooling around. I like the flower and candle touch. Reassures me that it's not a homicidal maniac using the place to stash his corpses."

Nice image. Now I've got something new to worry about. I ask if I should do anything.

"Make it obvious you're there," he tells me. "Not that you could help that."

I decide it's better not to ask what he means. "It's gorgeous out here," I tell him. "The setting, I mean. The furnishings are a crime. But the house is right on the water. I mean steps to it! And it's intimate. I can do incredible things with it." I can hear my voice rising with excitement. Even though Carmine has asked me to do the place in "that egg cruise" (as he insists on calling ecru), visions of shell colors are dancing in my head. I'll give him the shimmering pale beige, but I've got to have seashell pink. And white, white, white.

"Don't you mean *in* it? Incredible things *in* this intimate little love nest of yours?"

I remind him that it's not mine, but Carmine's, and that I'm here to work.

He says he guesses I'll be pretty busy working if I'm planning to get the job done in only four weeks. He offers to help on Thursday, his day off.

I don't want to sound too eager, so I tell him I've got it under control.

"What about all the furniture that's 'a crime?' You don't want me to investigate that?" When I'm silent, he adds, "And you're not worried about your intruders?"

I tell him that I wasn't when I was thinking of them as merely *trespassers*, at worst. "The back door was unlocked, so it's not like they broke in or anything," I say, sliding open the glass door and stepping out onto the patio. "I'd have used this place myself if I'd known it was here."

"No, you wouldn't," he tells me. "Law abiding people don't make themselves at home in houses that don't belong to them."

I don't say anything. I just wait.

"Unless they're invited," he adds, fishing.

What the hell? I figure, and go blithely after his line. "How about I do a barbecue on Thursday and you can invite Hal and his wife out, too." Drew's partner Hal thinks I'm a lunatic, and this seems like the perfect opportunity to prove to him that I am a serious businesswoman with real clients and that I'm good at what I do. "This could be the 'before,'" I say. "And in four weeks you can all come back for the 'after.'"

Drew asks if I'm sure I want to do that, like I'm playing with fire—and not in the grill.

"Tell them they'll have to bring bathing suits, their own towels, etcetera, because this place isn't really set up for guests yet. And I'll take care of the food."

Again he asks me if I'm sure this is a good idea. He reminds me that every encounter I've had with Hal has been a disaster.

"A day at the shore? Some beer, a few shrimp on the barbie.... What could go wrong?"

CHAPTER 3

Tuesday

Carmine De'Guiseppe stands with me in the middle of the living room, looking around. The man is well into his seventies and while he looks every hour of it around the eyes, the rest of him is what you might call jaunty. He sports a somewhat artificial tan and is wearing white pants, a white polo shirt and a navy blazer. All he's missing is a boat deck on which to stand.

His hair is snowy-white but very full, and his teeth are perfect when he smiles. He isn't smiling now, though.

"So you can fix it, right?" he asks hopefully. "Make it look—"

He stops himself midsentence and his fists ball. He mutters something about killing his sister as he uses the toe of one white loafer to lift the corner of the multicolored throw rug which covers the orange shag carpet. The corners of his mouth twitch as he grimaces.

"What you've gotta understand," he starts, looking out the glass doors as though he can see the ocean dancing behind the cinder block wall, "is that this place was gonna be special. It was like a dream, back then. A little piece of heaven off the beaten track."

"It's fixable," I tell him gently, touching his arm.

He pats my hand absentmindedly, and his eyes glisten. "I want that feeling back. You know what I mean? Whatever you need, you got. You understand me?" he asks.

I tell him I've worked out a budget and he nods his head and tells me, "Fine. Fine."

"All this furniture," he says, waving his hand, and I assure him that the Society of Saint Vincent de Paul is coming tomorrow. He tells me that his boys could get rid of it this afternoon, but I assure him that someone will make good use of it if we give it to St. Vincent's. "All *egg cruise*," he tells me, looking around.

"Ecru," I agree, nodding, thinking that once upon a time he had plans for this house, and that those plans probably included my mother. What will it hurt if I restore the place to what it was supposed to be? It's not like I'm handing him my mother on a silver platter, am I?

"You mind if I look around?" he asks.

I remind him that the place is his, not mine.

"You don't got anyone stashed in the bedroom?" he asks, and it takes me a minute to realize that he means a boyfriend and not a corpse.

I tell him that I haven't made the bed, but other than that, everything is pretty much the way I found the place. I'm about to tell him about the wine and the flowers, but he's wistfully tracing the hall wall with his finger on his way to the bedroom and I feel like I'd be ruining his memories, defiling his *piece of heaven*.

"Small," he says when he opens the bedroom door. He tries not to look at my messy bed, but there isn't much else to look at.

"Intimate," I correct, fussing with the coverlet until he stops me and swings an arm around my shoulder.

"You're a nice girl," he tells me, giving me a fatherly squeeze. "You know that?"

I think about how he saved Dana's bat mitzvah, showing up with a truck full of games and prizes and a band that the kids are still talking about at school. "You're a nice man," I say back to him. "You know that?"

He shakes his head. "Not as nice as you think," he says, letting go of his hold on me and turning to leave. "But not as bad, either."

I let him get several steps ahead of me before I leave the room and shut the door. I feel like I've stumbled into the man's dream. Or his memories. I've intruded somewhere I don't belong.

"The boys are coming out," he says, standing by the glass doors and talking to the beach. "Bringing a few things."

"Really?" I say, trying not to show my annoyance. I have a plan for the cottage and it doesn't include anything *the boys* might pick out. "Like what?"

He assures me it's just a few things, nothing I can't decorate around. "And only the best, top of the line," he adds.

It's his house, I remind myself. If he wants chandeliers in the bathroom, he can have them. If he wants ecru carpeting and walls and furniture, he can have it. Trying not to borrow trouble, I suggest a walk on the beach while we wait. I figure I can work on him out there, pitch some of my ideas with the ocean to back me up.

And I can always blame the surf for not hearing what he says.

Carmine looks out at the sunshine and down at his shoes. I open the sliding glass door and let the salty air work its magic. Slipping out the door I hold my hands out to him.

"Come on. I'll help you with your shoes and stuff."

He lets me pull him outside, sits while I take off his shoes and socks and roll up his pant legs. His skin is blue-white and cracked. Age spots compete with freckles for possession of his ankles.

I walk backwards, holding his hands as if I'm teaching him to ice skate. The wind whips at my hair and the fresh air fills my lungs. When we get to the wet sand, I let go with one hand and turn so that we face away from the sun together as we stroll down the beach.

"You see your friend the detective lately?" he asks me.

I tell him that I spoke to Drew last night. "I thought someone might have been in the house," I tell him, and feel him stiffen. I imagine his men watching me for the next four weeks, for my own protection. "But I was wrong. Just a neighbor taking out his garbage."

"You're locking the doors?" he asks me and I assure him that, with the exception of the bathroom door, which doesn't seem to unlock, of course I am.

"Has no one really been out here since the fifties?" I ask. "Because the place was pretty clean. Not much dust or anything, I mean."

He tells me that he hasn't been here since 1959, but that his sister was here for a while in the sixties.

"Does she still have a key?" I ask, trying not to fish too obviously. "I was going to have Mark change the locks and—"

Carmine tells me he wouldn't bother on her account. "Dead fifteen or sixteen years now," he adds just as we hear a truck horn and look up toward the house.

Now, it's been said that every emotion I've ever had is written on my face, so you can imagine what Carmine sees when I look up and see a lavender truck pulling up by the house and a burly arm waving to us.

"You'll like the stuff," Carmine says, putting both arms around me and hugging me tightly against him. "In fact, I guarantee you'll love it all or the boys'll take it back."

One of Carmine's men whistles loudly at us and makes some joke about taking that sort of stuff inside. Carmine doesn't think it's funny. He holds me close to him the whole way up the beach, only letting me go as we get to the road, where a cranberry-colored Camry speeds down the street, almost knocking us both down.

"Idiot!" he yells after the car.

Okay, he yells something worse, but that's close enough.

"You want us to—" the driver of the truck asks, gesturing toward the Camry's taillights.

Carmine shakes his head, indicating to let it go, and says what he wants is for Victor, the man riding shotgun (not literally…at least I hope not), to apologize to me, which I say is unnecessary.

He ignores me and asks Victor, "You think it's funny to embarrass her?"

"Let me see what you've brought," I pipe up, trying to sound enthusiastic.

The man puts his hand on the door handle, but Carmine

puts his palm against the door. He isn't strong enough to stop the guy from opening the door, but the guy stops anyway. And he apologizes.

"It did look, boss, like you two was…" He stops himself and tries to backpedal as fast as he can. "Not to me. I mean, I know how you…I mean, youse two…I don't mean to say…"

"Show me what you've brought," I say, and Carmine nods to the men, who jump out of both sides of the truck and open the back doors.

The most beautiful biscuit-colored Viking range and refrigerator I have ever seen in person are strapped to the walls of the van. My voice sticks in my throat.

"*Egg cruise*," Carmine says.

I don't correct him.

"Dishwasher's still in the carton," he says.

When I can find my voice I tell him that these appliances are for real cooks. I imagine the look on my friend Howard's face if he could see what I'm seeing. We'd need a beach towel for the drool.

"That's me," Carmine says, thumping his chest. The men around him agree heartily, one crediting him with the belly he is sporting.

"His manicotti, better than any restaurant you've ever been in," one of his boys says, and kisses his fingers in appreciation.

I must look skeptical, or amazed, but Carmine laughs and promises me a special dinner when the place is finished. "You and me, and maybe your mother would like to come," he says.

"My mother is on a cruise," I say. I don't know where it comes from, but out it pops. "Long cruise. Over a month. Far away."

"Really?" Carmine says, and I can't tell if he's disappointed or confused.

"I love this stove," I say, caressing its incredibly smooth enamel.

"We can store this stuff in the garage until you're ready to have it installed," Carmine tells me and I nod. "You been in there yet?" he asks.

I admit I haven't.

"The boys'll check it out," he says, gesturing to them.

"You want the bed in there?" one of them asks.

Carmine looks at me. "You think a king-size bed will fit?"

CHAPTER 4

Thursday

Mark shows up early. He is big and he is tan and he is what my mother would refer to as a "hunk." He flirts unabashedly with anything female, including Maggie May, and he is too young for me, and in a few years I will have to forbid him from asking Dana out because then I would have to kill him.

"You might have at least left something to sit on," he says, looking around at the nearly empty living room. "Where are we gonna neck? The floor?"

I explain that St. Vincent de Paul only comes out every other Wednesday, and so it was beach chairs on the sand or trip over the furniture while we paint. I opted for the chairs in the sand. And I remind him that Drew is coming today, which he claims is the only reason we aren't going to be necking on the beach.

I ignore his comment and point out that, of course, the sky is looking dark and threatening now because the cosmos always conspires to make me look like a jerk whenever I see Hal Nelson.

After sharing a muffin—hopefully he got the half with all the calories—we stroll over to the garage so that I can show him what we have for the kitchen. I am nearly jumping up and down in my flip-flops, telling him about the gorgeous new appliances, bashfully admitting that I hadn't realized the garage belonged to this house and not the neighbor's, when he throws open the door and the sunlight glints off the chrome. And also off a small mirror which sits atop a pile of clothes nestled beside what appears to be a makeshift bed.

"Oh, shit," Mark says.

"*Oh, shit* is right," I say. Maybe someone hasn't been sleeping in my bed, but they've sure been sleeping in my garage.

"Nice stove," Mark says, trying to ignore the little pile of belongings that doesn't belong here.

"We put the clothes outside, we lock the door, and we leave a note," I tell Mark, gathering up the two T-shirts and the little bikini.

"Can you put my cell number on that note?" Mark says, holding up the string bikini by one of its strings, from which dangle two small triangles.

I grab the suit away from him while he chuckles.

"She doesn't seem like a major threat," he says, and I have to agree. Anyone who could cover everything important with so little cloth isn't going to take me down in any fair fight.

I decide to leave a twenty-dollar bill along with the girl's stuff, and hope she buys food with it. Or a cover-up.

We lock up the garage and Mark asks where I want him to start. I tell him we've got to get down the wall by the patio. "In addition to blocking the incredible view that you buy a place like this for, I think that wall probably provided the opportunity for my little trespasser to come and go without being noticed."

He is on his way out the back door to examine the wall, but

that stops him in his tracks. "Your trespasser? Are you saying the kid's been inside?" he says, and I swear he gets larger as he says it. So large that he fills the door frame.

"It's no biggie," I tell him, not any happier with his over-reaction than Drew's casual one. "But yeah, I think whoever's sleeping in the garage was also coming into the house." I *know* she was, but I really don't want to make anyone else crazy. Just me is bad enough.

Mark fiddles with the sliding glass door, and fumes. "I'm putting new locks on this piece of crap door before I leave tonight," he says, glancing toward the front door and harrumphing. "And don't look at me like that. She might be little, but for all we know she's a strung-out junkie. Or her boyfriend is. Girl like that isn't alone for long, so until I've got a new lock in, you put a pole in the track of this door when you close it. I've got something in the truck you can use."

Now, instead of getting rid of the wall I want gone before my company shows up, he's intent on my locks. "Uh, all you've seen is her bra," I say, "and you've already got men panting to get into her panties—in my house."

Mark looks at me and I correct myself. "Carmine's house. The house I'm staying in. What difference does it make? Besides, I don't expect to be in jeopardy tonight. The locks can wait until tomorrow."

"I see," he says, shaking his head. "So I'm all wrong thinking that some man might want to get into some woman's panties. Excuse me for having such a dirty mind. Now can you please spell out for me why it is you won't be in jeopardy tonight?"

I get very busy examining holes in the walls.

"You know," Mark all but drawls, "I don't even want to hear it. And if you think having a man with a gun here with you makes me worry less about your safety, you aren't thinking straight."

"Are you suggesting I have to worry about Drew shooting me?" I mean, I know he doesn't trust Drew, but really.

"I'm suggesting that happiness isn't necessarily a warm gun, no matter what the Beatles said." He tosses this last comment over his shoulder as he heads out to his truck for some tools.

When he comes back in, he's carrying a small ladder which he sets down in front of me with a thump. He crosses his arms over his chest like some sort of genie and glares at me, gesturing toward the ladder like it's just implicated me in a record heist.

"What?" I ask before I choke on the smoke coming out of his ears.

"You're locking all your windows and doors every night, right?" he asks me.

Of course not. It's summer by the ocean. I have my windows open wide. I nod at him, anyway.

"And every time you leave the house, you lock up, right?" he adds. "'Cause finding this ladder leaned up under your bedroom window and knowing I'm not the one doing the peeping, isn't making me real happy. And it sure lends credence to the theory that our little woman in the itsy bitsy isn't necessarily alone."

Well, don't I feel naked? Exposed. Even if they are just kids. Ugh! I think of Jesse and Dana and their friends and six degrees of separation and someone knowing someone who's seen their mother dancing in the dark in her underwear with a glass of wine in her hand. "I was cleaning the windows," I lie.

Mark doesn't buy it for a minute. He asks if I have blinds on the bedroom window. I tell him I will after he installs the wooden shutters I've got on order. He wants to know what we're doing until then. "And please don't tell me that you'll be having police protection for the duration."

I tell him that Drew and his partner are coming out for a barbecue and that I don't know if Drew is staying overnight or not. I resist telling him it's none of his concern.

I have to give the man credit for merely muttering under his breath the lecture he'd like to give me. I remind him that I want the wall to come down, and he gives me the "yes ma'am, right away ma'am, anything you say ma'am," business as he bows and scrapes his way through the dining room and out the patio door.

While he sets up his equipment, I do what I can to get the place ready for Hal and his wife, which includes sweeping, cleaning and washing the dishes so that we can use them. But I don't do any decorating, since I want the place as dismal as possible. That way the difference will be really dramatic when they come back in four weeks. I only wish they could see the old furniture I had hauled out of here.

Mark turns on the portable radio that he always brings with him, and shouts more than sings in my direction. Kenny Chesney's "She's Got It All" is playing and I pretend I don't know every word, and that he isn't zinging my heart with his hammer.

I fill the sink with soapy water, thinking about someone peeking in at me while I danced or slept. I can't help shivering, and it doesn't help to tell myself that once they saw I was here, they left. I think leaving the ladder under the window was a message. Some sort of warning. Like they wanted me to know that they were here.

Mark startles me. "How low do you want the wall, beautiful?" he asks, and I jump several feet and drop the glass I'm holding. "You okay?"

I tell him that of course I am, though I'm standing in bare feet and there is now broken glass all over the kitchen floor. He crunches through it, lifts me up and deposits me in the living room with orders to "stay put." I've outgrown taking orders, so I slip on my flip-flops, take the broom from his hands and tell him I'll clean up the mess after we discuss the wall height. Seething, he follows me outside, where the blue sky is now gray and the ocean is beginning to whip up and send froth toward the beach.

At least that makes it cool for us to work. Which means Mark won't be taking off his muscle shirt.

Not that I care.

We decide that if we leave the wall at somewhere around twenty inches, we'll have the view plus a wall to sit on, as well. Mark stretches out his chalk line and we plunk it, leaving a line across the wall for him to follow. He picks up his sledgehammer and hits one cinder block above the line. From low in his throat comes "Oh, baby," as three blocks pop out. Only Mark can make taking down a wall seem sexy. "Piece of cake."

He takes another whack. And another. Chunks of the wall come down. He knows me well enough to offer me the sledgehammer and he holds out the handle to me with his usual warning to take care. Truth told, there's more than a bit of aggression I've worked out with Mark's tools.

I take a swing at the wall like I'm Barry Bonds without the steroids. A block goes flying, along with something else.

"What the heck was that?" Mark asks, as I hand him the hammer and go to pick up the black object resting ten feet away in the sand.

But I don't pick it up. I stare at it. I stare at it so long that Mark comes over and he looks down at it, too. He makes a sort of "hmph" noise and reaches for it.

"Careful," I warn him. "It could be loaded."

CHAPTER 5

"This thing's probably so rusted it'll be lucky to come up in one piece, never mind shoot," he says, but he handles the gun lying on the sand gingerly, nonetheless. And then his face is split by a grin. "I'll be damned. A Walther PPK."

Which sounds familiar to me. "Wait," I say. "Isn't that James Bond's gun?" I don't even know how I know that. It's one of those useless things that get stuck in your brain accidentally and won't come off, like gum on your shoe.

Mark is fondling the gun like you might imagine he'd fondle—if you let your mind go there, which I won't—a woman. It looks to be in pristine condition. Who knew burying something in a cinder-block wall would preserve it so perfectly?

"Why would someone bury a gun in a wall?" I ask, though I think we all know the answer.

"You're gonna tell me I have to give this to the police, aren't you?" Mark says, and he holds the gun against his chest protectively. "It's gotta be at least fifty years old, beautiful. And the only fingerprints on it now are bound to be mine."

I run back to the wall and look into the hollows of the blocks. There's something deep inside one and I stick my hand in as far as it will go. I grab the edge of something. Paper?

Thicker. A card? When I retrieve it, it turns out to be a faded photograph of a woman in a brief two-piece bathing suit, circa 1950. She is wearing a big sun hat which hides her face. Still, she looks alarmingly familiar. As the wind tries to take the photo out of my hands, I tell myself that all women in bathing suits from the fifties look alike.

Mark, still fondling the gun and humming the Beatles tune—about which he has clearly changed his mind—looks at the photo over my shoulder. "What's that?" he asks.

I tell him he has to carefully remove the cinder blocks one at a time so that we can search the crevices of each one. He reminds me that this job is supposed to be done in four weeks and that I have company coming. At which point I remind him that he gets paid by the hour. He replies something on the order of "it's your dime," and goes back to work. I, meanwhile, start looking through the blocks he's already removed. I find nothing.

"Those probably would have been too high for anyone to have stuck something in," Mark says, indicating the blocks I've searched. "Unless, of course, it was the guy building the wall."

Only we both know it wasn't him, right? I mean, this is Carmine De'Guiseppe's house, a house I never should have agreed to do.

Really, what was I thinking?

After another smack or two, Mark says, "Something's in here," but his hand is too big to get it out. I reach in and pull out a small wad of what appear to be letters. On the back of the pack is the word *love*, followed by a simple J. I hesitate to unfold the stack, and not because I'm afraid I'll destroy them. "Are they legible?" he asks.

I take a deep breath and screw my courage to the cinder blocks. Or place my butt there, anyway. The ocean is screaming in the background and the wind is now whipping up in earnest. I have to hold on to the letters with both hands or risk their being pulled out of my grasp and being lost forever.

Not necessarily a bad thing.

I unfold the pack of them and see that the words have faded badly, some to the point of oblivion. I brush the hair out of my eyes, but it immediately blows back across them while I try to make out the few words that have survived. A sentence fragment here: *differences in our religions, for one…* Another there: *the kind of life you lead…* And still another: *When love and duty cannot be reconciled…*

On the last page, hastily scrawled, are four separate words I can make out clearly: *police, protect, implicate* and *never.*

And the damn *J.* That's clear as a bell.

"Hello?" I hear from inside the house, and oh my God, Drew is here with Hal and what's-her-name, and all I can do is thrust the papers at Mark with a look that says *put them someplace safe and don't say a word.* With a nod, he acknowledges the message and a moment later the papers disappear. I think the gun is already in his pocket. That or he's uncharacteristically happy to see Drew. "Teddi? You out here?"

I wave hello, but the three of them stand just inside the doorway, peering out at me. Finally Drew comes over and takes my arm. "Anyone ever tell you that a beach is no place to be in a storm?" he asks.

"It's not exactly a storm," I answer, but my words are

drowned out by the rumble of thunder that precedes the first big splat of raindrops.

Mark gathers his tools quickly and hustles them into the house while Drew tries to hustle me in the same direction. There's no way I'm leaving the wall exposed to the elements, so I try to cover it with a tarp, holding down the edges with the discarded cinder blocks with Mark helping while Drew and his friends just gape at me in wonder. When I've got the wall covered, I turn to go into the house but the lawn furniture dances past me on my way.

"Chairs!" I shout at him, running after one that is tumbling down the beach just out of my grasp.

I grab it and carry it back to the house, bringing it and another one in, while Drew grabs the final two. I can see his lip twitching and I can't believe he's amused that it's raining on my parade.

I welcome Hal and his wife, whose name I can't for the life of me remember, and I apologize for the weather as if I'm responsible for it.

They react as if I am.

"Sorry about the chairs," I say. I explain about the Society of St. Vincent de Paul. Hal seems to think I'm making this up.

Mark makes some excuse about needing to get some supplies and using the rain as a good time to get them. He says he can just run up to Parsons Girl's Hardware and then be back tomorrow. "You have the paint swatches?" he asks as he follows me into the bedroom with a swagger that implies he's already been there.

And maybe done that, too.

In the bedroom he asks me what I want him to do with the gun. Of course, Drew overhears.

"What gun?" he asks, taking in the bedroom and cringing just a little at the accommodations. Wait until I've got the king-size bed installed...and nothing else. I bet he'll like it better then.

"It's a color," I say, though I am the world's worst liar. "You know, gunmetal gray?" I tell Mark it's for a different job, and he looks at Drew like he's daring him to call me on it.

"It involves my mother," I add, because that's the truth, and I am so much better with the truth than I am with lying.

And because I know that then Drew will just roll his eyes, which he does, and back off. He's had enough dealings with my mother and her fake kidnapping, her ring stealing, and all her other shenanigans to know that when it comes to June Bayer, he just doesn't want to know.

Which, at the moment, is fine with me. I mean, what if my mother impeded an investigation? Tampered with evidence? I watch *CSI*. I know there's no statute of limitation on murder. What about accessory to a murder? My mother's great with accessories...provided, of course, that the murder was committed in a taupe room.

If there was a murder, I remind myself. The saying is "where there's smoke, there's fire," not "where there's a gun, there's a corpse."

I look down at the floor. If the gun was in the wall, could the body be...

"...lunch?" Drew asks. Mark says thanks anyway, so I'm guessing Drew asked if he was staying and Mark's pretending it's an invitation. The two don't get along well. Not since Drew tried to arrest Mark for locking my front door. Well, he tackled him for that. Technically, he wanted to arrest him for marrying his housekeeper's daughter…which is a whole other story.

"Maybe we should just go out," I hear Hal's wife say, and I rush past Mark and Drew to find Hal trying unsuccessfully to get comfortable in a folding aluminum chair in the living room.

"Oh, I'm sure the rain will pass," I say, having never had a beach house and having no experience with summer storms at the shore. "It always does."

Hey—it wasn't raining yesterday, so the last storm passed, didn't it?

Drew joins us in the living room, leaving Mark in the bedroom alone. A moment later he comes out and winks at me. He makes a gesture, one hand sliding under the other, that I take to mean the gun and papers are under my mattress. That or it's a new way to flip someone the bird.

"Drinks!" I say brightly as I wave Mark off. I've got stuff for Mohitos, daiquiris and margaritas. I've got booze and salt and even little paper umbrellas for the beachyness of it all. "What can I get you, Holly?" I ask Hal's wife.

"Hallie," she corrects me, and sighs, clearly no more enamored with me than her husband is. "He's Hal, I'm Hallie. It's easy."

It should be. Of course, when you've just found out that your mother may be an accomplice to murder, nothing is really easy, is it?

"Got any lemonade?" she asks.

Of course I don't. But I've got lemons, and I can make some, which I offer to do.

"I'll just have a Pepsi," she says, resigned.

I've got Coke. I pray she isn't like Bobbie and that she won't be able to tell the difference.

Hal says he'll have a beer. "But none of that fancy imported stuff," he calls out after me.

Drew follows me into the little kitchen where there really isn't room for both of us. "Do I look like a grocery store?" I hiss at him. This he takes to correctly mean that I have Heineken and not Schlitz.

"Calm down," he tells me, a phrase I hate almost as much as "What's your mother done now?"—which, thankfully, he doesn't ask.

From nowhere he pulls out a little insulated tote that's filled with Coors and Pepsi. I can't decide if I should be grateful or pissed that he anticipated my need to be rescued.

Hal's wife stands in the doorway and asks for directions to the "little girls' room." I want to tell her that only grown ups are allowed to pee here, but instead I point and warn her that the door is fussy and she shouldn't pull it tightly closed. She gives me an exasperated look.

"You know if the stove works?" Drew asks me, pretending that he doesn't have the world's most obnoxious partner and that Hal doesn't have the world's most obnoxious wife.

"You really don't think the rain will stop?" I ask, opening the beer and the Pepsi and pouring them into glasses, while Drew takes a Heineken out of the fridge and uses the edge of the counter to pop off the top.

"Not today," he says, playing with a paper umbrella and trying to stick it in my hair, which I realize is still a disaster from the wind. He puts the stem to the umbrella in his beer bottle and follows me out of the kitchen.

"Hal," I say, handing him his Coors. "Haley," I say, handing her the Pepsi.

"Hallie," she corrects, while shooting a look at Hal.

Whatever, I think. "Right. Sorry."

"What's with the wall?" Hal asks, gesturing toward the sliding doors.

I explain that I'm having it knocked down, leaving a roughly two-foot-high ledge for people to sit on, while restoring the view.

"What the hell did they build the wall there for in the first place?" he asks.

To hide evidence doesn't seem like the best answer when it's a cop asking the question. "Privacy, I suppose," works better.

"Who needs that much privacy?" Hal asks.

"Cops are notoriously suspicious," Haley/Hollie/Whoever says, and studies her toenail polish and bites the inside of her cheek.

"Only when there's something to be suspicious about," her husband says pointedly, like she's supposed to know what he means.

Which, if the glare is any indication, she does. She slams her glass of Pepsi down on the floor beside her chair, soda sloshing over the side, and stares at the cracks in the ceiling.

"Nice," Hal says, though I wave away the mess.

"So," I say brightly. "What were we talking about?"

"Suspicion," all three of them say in unison as if daring me to make lemonade out of that lemon.

"Well," I blabber, trying to defuse the situation. "You guys see so much unjustice…*in*justice, I mean. Being cops, that is. You see the underbelly of…badness."

Hal just stares at me. I try smiling at him. I have a really great smile, or so I'm told, and it usually wins people over and they respond well. Hal doesn't. He shifts in the lawn chair and grimaces, just in case I thought he was comfortable.

"Well, this will be an adventure," I say. I have to raise my voice because the rain is pelting the windows and the roof. I think about the letters and hope Mark has them in a dry place.

"So do you know if the stove works?" Drew asks me again.

Actually, I have no idea what he asks. I'm thinking about the photo and the letters and if my mother could be *J*, and if she was in this house, and if she and Carmine, right here, in the bed I'm sleeping in…

I excuse myself and slip into the bedroom, where I call Mark and ask if the letters are safe. He assures me they and the gun are under the mattress, just as I thought. Then I ask him what he and Drew said before he left. "I asked him if I needed to come back to change the locks tonight," he tells me.

"And?"

Drew pops his head into the bedroom. "Great hostessing," he tells me, sarcasm dripping. "I'm gonna light the stove."

I nod at him, and what he says takes a minute to register. Actually it doesn't register until I smell the plastic bun wrappers burning.

I hang up on Mark, who never does tell me Drew's response, and I run out of the bedroom to find all my guests in the kitchen bumping into each other trying to get the bag of buns out of the oven and into the sink.

"I bet these things happen to you all the time," Hal's wife says. I like her even less than I like Hal, who says something about my house smelling like a barn full of bull farts.

In the midst of this, my mother calls—my cell phone playing the theme from *Looney Tunes*—and Hal bursts into mean-spirited guffaws. He is still talking about how appropriate my ringer is long after I have gotten off the phone with my mother, who suddenly wants to know whose house I am doing and where exactly it is.

She and my father have decided to come out and advise me. Which is just perfect since I have a sneaking suspicion that the reason Carmine wants an "egg cruise" house is in the hope that my mother will be there. And now, lo and behold, it appears she will be. I somehow do not think this is what Carmine has in mind.

The whole June/Carmine thing was bad enough before I got myself in the middle of it. I'm about to say that parents should be too old for sex when I realize I am one.

Hal makes some nasty crack about contingency plans. Okay, it's not a nasty crack. He just asks what they are. What I'd had in mind in the event of rain.

It's clear I had nothing in mind. And here we are, sheets of rain coming down, an oven with burnt plastic on the racks, three hungry guests and one maniac hostess with a possible felon for a mother.

Haley suggests again that we go out to eat. "We can't stay here," she says, like *here* is a sinking boat in the middle of the Indian Ocean during typhoon season.

Hal, who has disagreed (and dismissed) everything his wife has said, asks if I have a few decks of cards. When I admit that

I don't know, he starts opening and closing drawers in the breakfront and I panic.

I start shouting about an invasion of my client's privacy and something about lack of search warrants and the only thing that saves me from making a complete and total ass of myself…well, nothing really saves me from *that*, but what saves me from going on and on is that the lights flicker twice and then go out.

At least that gets rid of Hal and Hallie, whose name I botch up three more times as they are leaving.

When I finally shut the door and lean against it, Drew and I are both laughing.

"Okay, he could have been nicer about it," Drew says. "It's not like you made it rain."

By this he means that the oven fiasco was my fault, as was the lack of comfortable seating, no food, etc. I find the whole thing too funny to argue about. I stop laughing when Drew asks me about the gun.

I try playing dumb, but he doesn't buy it. You'd think after today he'd have no trouble believing I'm just a blithering idiot.

"I can show you the color on my calibrated color chips," I offer.

"Your mother gave you a gun, didn't she?" Drew says.

I love it when I can tell him honestly that he's mistaken.

"Your mother is involved, which means it has nothing to do with gray color chips," he tells me. "So what does your mother have to do with a gun?"

I never thought I'd be praying for lightning to strike the house I'm standing in.

CHAPTER 6

Thursday night

"The case is over fifty years old, if it even is a case," Drew says after I've demonstrated that my ability to keep a secret is almost as good as my ability to make contingency plans for dinner parties. "But I'll take the gun in."

It seems to me that if he takes the gun in to the locals, they will have to open a file. Since I don't really want that to happen, I rely on the cover of darkness and tell him I threw it in the ocean.

"Really?" he asks, but he apparently couldn't care less, because I see his silhouette shrug, and then he tells me to bring a blanket into the living room so that we can cuddle on the floor while we watch the lightning.

Okay, he doesn't say *cuddle*, but there really isn't any need to be crude here, is there? I mean, we all know what he has in mind.

So I drag the cotton comforter in from the bedroom, tripping on it and nearly winding up in his lap prematurely.

"Eager?"

He should only know the half of it. If I was any more eager

I'd have peeled his clothes off when he walked in the door—
Hal and Hallette notwithstanding.

I ask him if he doesn't want to see the letters. "Can't see in
the dark," he says, expertly finding the clasp to my bra. "Gotta
feel my way."

I offer no resistance.

"They're all signed *J*," I tell him. "As in June."

He's doing incredible things to the hollow of my throat.
"And Jennifer," he mumbles. "Also Judy, Joan, Joanne, Jean,
Jeanette…need I go on?"

"Go lower," I say.

"Julie, Justine." He's licking his way down my chest. "Then
we hit the K's."

He latches on to my nipple and bites it gently. "Stop at the
K's," I say, my voice gravelly.

"You sure? There's Lois," he says, his tongue tickling my ribs.
"Mary," he says, tugging on my shorts.

"Holy, Mary!" I say when his fingers creep up the inside of
my thigh and slip within my undies and then some.

"Nancy. Norma." Tongue still sliding down, now tracing my
belly button and heading farther south.

"Now!" I say, arching.

"Paula." A kiss closer to his exploring hands. "Rita."

"Right there!" I arch against his assault.

"Sally. Sharon…" His words get muffled against me.

"Shut up," I say.

"But I'm just getting to the best one," he says, pulling me
into position. "Teddi, Teddi, Teddi." He licks me once. Twice.
"Only Teddi."

And then he's done with the words, and I'm murmuring incredible sounds. Things like "Oh, yes! Oh, yes! Yes! Yes!" and "There! There!"

And even with my eyes closed I can see the bolts of lightning turning the sky to daylight and releasing it back to blackness again. And then he swings me out from under him and seats me low on his belly. And I arch back and open my eyes wide and the thunder claps and the lightning crackles and…

…and there is someone outside the patio door, face pressed to the glass. I scream and jump off Drew, who whips around a moment too late.

"Someone was looking in," I tell him, covering myself with the blanket. "A girl I think. Or maybe a young boy, watching us."

Drew gets up slowly. Sadly. "Probably just hoping to get in out of the storm. In all likelihood, your trespasser's a runaway."

"She shouldn't be out there in this," I say, suddenly more concerned for her than for myself. After all, I'm safe and dry here with Drew.

"You want me to look for her, don't you?" he says, resigned as he slips into his jeans. "You want me to go out there and…"

He stops when we see a light in front of the house and hear an engine start. He parts the front curtains and we watch red taillights trailing down the block.

"Not too many runaways with cars," I say.

"Not with late-model Camries, anyway," he says. "Couldn't catch the plate in the rain."

A *Camry*, I think, and bells and whistles go off. "I think she wanted me to see her," I say. "Why else would she be smack in the middle of the glass doors?"

"It's not like she wasn't getting an eyeful there," he says. "Looks like your carpenter friend is right about you having a Peeping Tom."

"A Peeping Tom who left pizza in the fridge and flowers on the table? Is that SOP for a PT?"

"PT?" he asks. "Oh. Peeping Tom. I get it." Apparently that's not what the police call it, but he doesn't tell me what they refer to it as.

"Aren't you going to call anyone?" I ask.

"Like…?"

"The police?" I say, realize that of course, he *is* the police, and then say that I mean the local police.

"Sure. I'll call and say some kid was out in the rain and he looked into the house my friend was decorating and saw me with my head between your thighs—"

He looks at me.

"What?" he asks. Like he doesn't know what he just called me. *Friend?* I'm thinking. *Is your head usually found between your friend's thighs?* But there is no way I'm going to say that, so I make up something about my mother and the letters and photo and gun, and Drew isn't the least bit interested. He manages to throw a sheet up over the window and then locates a corkscrew and a bottle of wine—all in the darkness.

He pours us each a glass and settles back down on the floor, putting up his hand to guide me down next to him.

"Now," he says. "Where were we?"

CHAPTER 7

Friday morning

In the morning, Drew goes up to Joanne Guest's place for some fresh pastries and coffee—Bobbie isn't the only one who thinks I don't make a decent cup—while I call my mother.

She answers on the first ring. "Did you find a husband yet?" she asks.

I tell her I've been here all of four days and that I'm working.

"Five, but who's counting?" she responds. "And working on what? That house? Or solving the real problems in your life? No doubt you're hanging out with that contractor of yours. The hunky one who's young enough to date Dana and probably doesn't have a pot to pee in."

I tell her Mark and I aren't "hanging out." We're working. She doesn't sound impressed. She should only know who I *am* hanging out with….

"And no Detective *Spoonshorts*, either," she says like she can read my mind.

I tell her I've got too much work to do to even think about men.

"Four weeks, Teddi, and one is almost used up. What are you going to do if you don't meet someone out there?"

I swear she asks this, and she is serious.

"I'm going to collect my well-earned check, sign it over to my children, go back home and put my head in the oven," I tell her.

She tells me not to joke about such a thing, and I automatically apologize. There is a lapse in the conversation and then she says, "Your father and I are coming out there tomorrow."

Great. I'm nearly two hours from my home and still everyone I know is dropping in like I'm just down the block. At this rate I'll get the house finished for New Year's. "Mom, I was only joking. You don't have to come check on me."

"It isn't always about you," she snaps at me. "I haven't been out to the Hamptons in ages. I want to see how the place has changed."

Well, for starters, there's a wall missing....

She expects an argument, but she doesn't get one. Seeing her see this house could answer a lot of questions. I ask if she has a pen to take down the directions.

"Just e-mail them to your father," she says. "He's always on that damn computer anyway. At least an e-mail from you won't cost us anything."

Instead of asking what she means, which is what she wants me to do, I tell her that my computer isn't hooked up yet, and I only have dial-up out here anyway, so would she please get a pen?

"He goes to porno sites," she says. "And not even the free ones."

"A pen?" I repeat. Hey, if my suspicions are correct, she shouldn't be throwing any stones at my father.

She says she'll get my dad, and I tell her that since she's familiar with the Hamptons, she should listen in, too. What I really want to know is if she's the woman in the photo, the one who wrote the notes signed *J*, and if she knows how the gun got in the wall.

But I know better than to ask her straight out. She's like one of those animals that you have to approach sideways, sneak up on them without entering their radar zone or something. Because if there's a way out, they—and my mother—will find it.

"The place is on Foam View," I say, listening for a gasp. Of course, it's possible that over the years the name's been changed. Back in the fifties most of the roads out here were simply route numbers.

With the hope of jogging her memory, I tell her to take Route 25A, claiming it is more scenic and interesting—words she claims are code for *tedious* and *slow*.

They'll be coming via the Long Island Expressway, she says.

Not much chance a route that didn't exist back then will jog her memory.

"Fine. When you get to Riverhead, you can pick up…" and on I go, listening for any signs of recognition. I hear none until Drew comes back in the front door and calls out my name.

That she recognizes.

"No wonder you haven't found a husband," she says. I tell her she's right. Until Drew showed up I was beating them off with a stick.

She hangs up on me.

Drew wants to play, but my mother is right that the number of days I've got left is dwindling, and I tell him that we've got to rip up the carpeting before Mark gets here with the paint for the walls.

As I start to ease off the baseboard molding with a pry bar, I hear Drew's cell phone ring. Three minutes later he's giving me a peck on the cheek and promising to call when he gets the chance.

"But this is fun," I try, figuring if it worked for Tom Sawyer, maybe it'll work for me. "The surf pounding outside, us pounding inside…"

"I thought you wanted to pull up the carpeting," he says, pretending I've just propositioned him, which, if Mark wasn't due here any minute, I'd consider doing. He takes my chin in his hand and looks disappointed, which does make me feel a little better. "Gotta go," he says with a shrug.

He examines the doorknob on his way out.

"Lock this behind me," he says, and I nod, but don't get up. I check my watch and it's nearly nine. Mark will be here in just a couple of minutes. Which reminds me that he needs to fix the light switch in the hall and the knob on the bathroom door.

I get all the baseboards off and decide to wait for Mark to help me pull up the carpeting. If the carpet installers used those tack strips, I'll need a hand. I grab my cup of coffee and slide open the door to the ocean. *Come out and play*, it calls. *Come out and play.*

"I can't," I tell it silently, taking two steps out onto the patio to smell the salty air and fill my lungs.

Come wiggle your toes, the sand says.

"I can't," I say aloud, surprising myself. "I have work to do." I'm still holding the pry bar, and I put it down on the tarp which we flung over the remains of the wall yesterday.

Just dip one toe, the water says.

And what do I say? Do I stick to my guns, so to speak? Do I pull the tarp off the cinder blocks to see if it's hiding any more secrets?

No.

I say, "Oh, hell!" and race toward the water, the wet sand scattering in clumps as I run.

Shore birds, maybe they are sandpipers, skitter away and then come back, investigating me, wondering if I'm friend or foe.

"No dog," I tell them, wishing now that I'd brought Maggie May with me. "Just one crazy lady who ought to be inside working."

Yesterday's clouds are all gone. The sky is deep blue. The seagulls are screaming. When the water hits my toes, it is icy cold.

Someday, when I am rich and famous, I will have a beach house. Or at least I'll rent one for the summer. Okay, okay. So in the event that that day never comes to pass, I solemnly pledge to myself that for the next three weeks I will come out here every morning and soak up this feeling so that, some dark day in February when the snow is dirty and the kids are stir crazy and the driving is dangerous, I can recall the smell of the ocean and hear the waves lapping at my feet.

I walk up the beach, accompanied by the birds for a while, who dance at the water's edge, stopping only to investigate a bit of crab shell here, a bubbling hole there.

Mine are the only footprints on the beach and I am inordinately proud of my high arches, like having them is the result of having done something right.

But it doesn't take long for the guilt to catch up and overtake me. If the fog comes on little cat's feet, what does the guilt come on? Sandpiper's long legs? At any rate, I'm too calm and too content for a Jewish girl and so I turn and walk back toward the house, blinded by the sun's low position on the horizon.

In the distance, I hear Mark already hammering, and I quicken my step, embarrassed that I've abandoned my work ethic so early in the day.

As I turn from the ocean and head up the beach, the hammering stops. By the time I've gotten my pry bar and slid open the glass door, the house is silent as a tomb. Okay, in light of the notes and the gun, I don't really like that image, and I aim for something more benign.

"Mark?" I call out. The house is deathly quiet. Oops. There I go again. "Mark?" I try louder. "Quit kidding!"

At the front of the house, I pull back the blinds, expecting to see Mark's truck. Only it isn't there.

I change my grip on the pry bar I used to take off the moldings, holding it like a weapon even though I know that a large chipmunk could probably disarm me and you aren't supposed to wield a weapon someone could use on you. But I don't have a spoon handy. Anyway, I notice...

I notice...

What I notice is that the moldings I removed this morning are right back where they were to begin with. Attached to the walls. As if I'd never taken them off.

Now, two years ago my ex-husband, Rio, tried to make me think I was crazy by undoing things I did and doing things I didn't and telling me that I was responsible for all sorts of stuff—something for which I'll never forgive him. He had me so convinced that after he tricked me into shooting him with his own paint gun, I actually let myself be committed to South Winds Psychiatric Center.

So the idea that I could have not done something I distinctly remember doing doesn't sit well with me.

Grabbing up my cell, I dash out the front of the house. My first thought is to call Drew. After all, he saw me taking off the first baseboard. Right. Just recalling that calms me down.

Like that scene in *Gone With the Wind*, when Scarlett raises her fist and swears she'll never be hungry again, I raise mine and swear that I'll take that Walther PPK and hunt Rio down if he is behind this.

And I'll blame it on James Bond.

Maybe Dana's right and I'm watching too many old movies.

"Rio?" I say when he answers his home phone.

"You were expecting someone else?" he says. "Whadja hit the wrong button, Teddi? Probably don't really want me, do you?"

"Where are you?" I demand, which I realize is stupid because I've called him at home, so where else could he be? And I hear the baby he and his wife have named Elisa (even though our youngest is called Alyssa) in the background, to boot.

"Teddi? Something the matter with the kids?" he asks, and I can tell that he is genuinely concerned. At least I think he is. Rio has played me so many times I could be a Stradivarius. Or at least a plastic ukulele.

"The kids are fine," I say. A bolt of brilliance hits me. "You still have that job Carmine got you with the security systems company?"

"What? You think I can't hold a job if I'm not married to

the boss's daughter?" he asks. Clearly I have caught him in a bad mood. And, because I know how liars operate, having been married to one for twelve years, I don't take this answer to mean he still has his job.

I ask him again, point blank. "Do…you…still…have…the job…Carmine…got…you?"

He drawls it out just as slowly. "Yes…I…do."

I tell him that I am doing a house in the Hamptons and want to have a security system installed. "Video, the whole nine yards," I say.

He hems and haws and tells me it's a big trip out to the Hamptons and he'll have to charge me travel time. I tell him he isn't charging me a thing because the work is for Carmine De'Guiseppe.

"Right," he says, like I'm making it up. Talk about the pot calling the kettle black.

I ask him who is in charge of lying in our family, anyway.

He reminds me we aren't a family.

I can't believe I've called us one. I am so utterly appalled at myself that I am just staring at the phone when Mark pulls up.

I thrust my cell at him. "Tell him he has to be here at seven tonight, that no one can know what he's doing here, and that he better do it right or he'll be swimming with the fishes."

Mark looks at me. He looks at the phone. He smiles and takes it out of my hand. "Drew?" he says into the phone. "I think you really pissed her off this time."

MARK CHANGES all the outside locks and adds dead bolts. He is disappointed that it isn't Drew I'm ticked at. And he isn't any happier that my ex-husband is coming over tonight. In fact, he offers to stay around while Rio does his work. But while Rio is no longer any sort of temptation, Mark is. And I have no intention of ruining a great working relationship just for one damn good cry, a dynamite little back rub, a little imported wine—and then the inevitable roll in the hay.

Or on the sand.

I remind him that he has to get home to Maggie and he re-assures me that the dog is doing fine without me. How nice to know that all this time it's just been an illusion that she or the kids need me at all.

By the time Rio pulls up, somewhere after eight, Mark is gone and I am now four full days behind schedule. And instead of getting a primer coat on the living room walls, I have spent the last hour watching the house from the beach to catch whoever is entering it and messing with my mind. I see no one until Rio circles the house looking for me.

Because I don't want my stalker, or whatever she is/they are, to know I'm about to catch her/them on tape, I wave to Rio like he's a long-lost friend and not a security systems expert.

He waves back cautiously, clearly suspicious. Maybe he doesn't know he's an expert, either.

I come up the beach to meet him. Damned if the man hasn't gotten even handsomer with age.

I, on the other hand, have put on four pounds and devel-oped a crow's foot by my left eye.

"You ought to have the sun behind you all the time, sort of bathing you in sunlight," he tells me.

"The sun is just about set," I respond, but I'm standing a

little straighter when I say it, and I can't help brushing the hair out of my eyes and hoping the wind catches it and spreads it alluringly behind me. *I made a big mistake*, I want him to think. *I was a fool.*

"I know," he says. "You're kinda backlit. You know, in silhouette. You really never did know how beautiful you are. I wish…"

The man has been practicing, damn him.

"How's Marion?" I ask, putting my arm around his waist like a sister and walking him toward the house. "And the baby?"

He takes the opportunity to let his hand roam down my back and insinuate itself into my back pocket. He could be fondling me or trying to rob me. One is as likely as the other with Rio.

Once we're inside, he pulls his hand back and asks what the show was all about and I wind up having to thank him for appearing so happy to see me.

"I am happy to see you. I'm always happy to see you," he says, and his hips thrust forward ever so slightly, giving greater meaning to his words.

Once upon a time, all this worked on me and I thought Rio Gallo was perhaps the sexiest man on earth. Just because it doesn't work on me now doesn't mean he isn't still up there with Brad Pitt and that guy from *Grey's Anatomy*.

Taking several steps back, intent on keeping my distance and making sure he keeps his, I tell him that strange things have been happening at the house. That there has been an intruder or a trespasser but that nothing has been stolen. In fact, after I found the baseboards replaced this morning, I found two lamps that I'd thrown out returned to the nightstands in the bedroom.

Rio does that woo-woo noise and asks if we haven't been here before. Then it occurs to him that I could be accusing him, and he swears he isn't responsible.

"Last time, yes," he says. "I mean, some of the stuff, anyway. But it was just because I was worried that you'd lose it in front of the kids if I didn't—"

I cut him off. This time I don't think he has anything to do with what's going on. He's relieved. And now he's Mr. Solicitous. "That's really scary," he tells me. "I don't like the idea of someone coming and going with you here all alone."

I tell him I'm not alone here much.

"Is someone going to be here with you tonight?" he asks, and he's trying to look deep into my eyes.

I give lying another try. I figure that practice makes perfect. "On top of company," I say, "I've got new locks. And I'll have your brand-new, up-to-the-minute, high-tech security system."

"Guess I better get to work, then," he says, but he doesn't seem to be moving in that direction. "I'd ask you if you want some dinner, but I bet you'll lie about eating, too."

I say I had a late lunch, hoping one o'clock qualifies.

We agree to order in a pizza, "like the old days," he says.

Great dieting technique—I lose my appetite.

I suggest he get started so that he can be done at a reasonable hour. He goes out to his car and comes back with brown grocery sacks full of wires and boxes and I watch him set up to install his security system.

The last time he installed cameras it was in my bathroom and he was hoping to get nude pictures of me to sell to *Playhouse Magazine* for an article on *Long Island's Most Dangerous*

Decorator. Back then he didn't realize that he had to connect the camera to something, but now he moves with grace and efficiency and seems to know exactly what he's doing.

When he has everything laid out, our pizza arrives and we eat it on the aluminum chairs on the patio. He takes two slices of pizza and stacks them, reminding me of John Travolta in *Saturday Night Fever*. Rio has always reminded me of John Travolta. I used to say that God was just practicing on JT and when he got it right, he made Rio.

Now I know why cloning should be forever illegal.

I pick at some pizza crust, but I don't want to eat with Rio. No breaking bread with the enemy. He reaches into the bag that came with the pizza and hands me a garlic knot I didn't order.

"Your favorite," he tells me.

"Developed an allergy," I say, but his look says he doesn't buy it. Then again, I'm hungry, and I'm not sure what the point of starving myself is, especially when I might need my strength later. Light-headed around Rio Gallo is not something I want to be.

Because we don't know who might be listening, we avoid talking about the reason for his visit and talk about the kids, and his work and mine. It is the most civilized discussion we have had since the day Bobbie and her sister Diane and I put all the pieces together and figured out that Rio had been *Gaslighting* me, just like Charles Boyer had done to Ingrid Bergman in the movie, and it had almost worked. I really was on the verge of going crazy.

I remind myself of all this while we chat amiably because if I forget for one second that Rio is the scum of the earth, even if he is my children's father, then maybe I'll start to trust him again, and that's a slippery slope I am not willing to go down.

"So, you still seeing that cop?" he asks me after a while. I figure it would be good for the intruder to know that I've got a cop visiting me, looking after me, and so I tell Rio he was here last night.

"He stay over?" Rio asks. His eyebrows lower as though he is expecting a blow.

"How're things with Marion?" I ask instead of answering. He has no right to ask me personal questions anymore, and I have no obligation to answer them.

Apparently he feels the same way, because he switches the conversation to the kids.

"She reminds me so much of Dana, when she was a baby," he tells me about the child he and Marion have. "You'd think it would be Alyssa, what with the name being so close and all, and how she was our last little one. But no, it's Dana."

"It's the dark eyes," I say. I was struck by how much Elisa looked like she could have been one of mine, myself. But then, Marion looks a lot like a younger version of me.

Rio takes two more slices of pizza, again stacking them.

"So you're really serious about this guy?" Rio asks after a while.

"We really ought to go in," I say. "It's getting buggy out here."

"You know, don't you, that I'd give, like, my right arm, to change it all, right?" he says. "I mean, you do know, right?"

I think before I answer him. Two years ago I'd have given anything to erase what Rio did and have us be one happy family again. Now? Not so much. I'm proud of having survived. I'm proud of my business and my friendships and my self-reliance.

I tell him that he has his life and I have mine, and that he'd better get going on the work he's promised to do for me.

He goes inside and I sit by myself for a few minutes trying to imagine what I'd be doing right now if my life hadn't taken the turn it did. There might be another baby. If Rio had convinced me to have just one more, I'd have never gone back to school. Another baby...

"This usually takes two people," he says at the door. "You wanna come help me?"

I get up reluctantly and he slides the glass door open. There's something different about Rio tonight. Something vulnerable. The cockiness is gone.

Ironically, it makes him more dangerous. I wish he'd hurry and finish. Even more ironic, I remember thinking that same thing in another context, having spent half the night up with a sick child and wishing for sleep.

"Teddi?" he says, and I jump at his touch. "I want to come home."

"You're dreaming," I tell him, brushing past him and picking up the ends of the wire he's left on the floor. "You've got a family. You set all this in motion, and now you've got to live with the consequences."

"I made a mistake," he says.

"Yeah," I agree. "Me, too. And I lived with mine for twelve years. Now you're gonna have to live with yours."

His shoulders sag. He can't look me in the face.

"Oh shit," I say.

He nods.

"She left you." It's not a question. "But I heard the baby when I called...."

He nods again.

"She left you *and* the baby?" I ask. My voice squeaks.

"We could—" he starts.

I back away from him like he's carrying one of those terrorist germ things. Ricin. Anthrax.

"You know how you love kids, and you just said how much she looks like—"

I put my hands over my ears and hum.

"My mother's taking care of her in the day," he shouts. He knows I think his mother is the worst influence a child could have to bear.

"Finish the job and get out," I say, running from the room.

"I don't feel right about leaving you alone here tonight," he says as I hurry into the bedroom and shut the door. "I'm just worried about your safety, Ted."

"Get out," I shout again, only it's muffled because I'm lying on the bed with the pillow pressed against me, imagining that poor baby spending her formative days with Mother Teresa Gallo whose name proves that even the Catholic God has a sense of humor.

"I'll just sleep on the couch," he says. "I swear."

Then he must look around, because he adds that the floor is fine.

I push myself off the bed and open the door a crack.

"My parents will be here first thing in the morning. And Mark, and there's this Walther PPK, so you'd better be gone and—"

"A Walther PPK? Really?" I hear him say. "Whose? Because you know how much you can get for one of those things?" And for the first time all evening he sounds like his old self.

Which is good, because now I want to kill him.

CHAPTER 8

Saturday

Rio—kiss the air and thank my lucky stars—leaves before my parents show up. I think he's more afraid of facing my father than the Walther PPK, though he does seem sorry he is going to miss that. I suppose that's what accounts for his being gone when I come out of the bedroom—the thought of my father and a Walther PPK in the same vicinity.

Mark rolls in around nine and calls me *Beautiful*. This despite the fact that I look like death warmed over because, instead of sleeping, I spent the night looking out my window for someone looking in, and making sure I didn't fall asleep and risk waking up with Rio in my bed.

He asks me how things went and I show him the security cameras.

"Wasn't asking about the job," he says with a grimace, like I've purposely misunderstood him.

"Nothing else to report," I say. I tell him Rio did his job and left. He looks suspicious, but he drops it.

The chaises I've ordered for the deck have arrived and he helps me unwrap them so that we can temporarily use them in the living room. The couch I've ordered won't show up for at least another week and this way company will have a place to sit.

When we're done, Mark sets up his table saw out back and totes out some strips of molding, while I make what passes for coffee. He flicks on his radio and flicks off his shirt. Remember those great Pepsi commercials where the girls in the office are watching the clock and then they all run to the window to watch when the construction worker takes off his shirt, tips his head back and drinks the soda straight out of the can?

Well, I'm getting the live version. And my construction guy is singing along with Brad Paisley that to him I am the world.

And did I mention he has his shirt off? Oh, I did?

Well did I mention that the surf is pounding behind him? And that the sun is glinting off his wraparound sunglasses?

Before you get too excited, did I also mention that my mother is bursting through the front door with my father in tow behind her? And that he is carrying her *suitcase?*

Suddenly, tying a cinder block to my ankle and jumping into that pounding surf is looking pretty good.

My mother tips her sunglasses and gets an eyeful of Mark. "That," she says, "should be illegal."

My father drops the suitcase to the floor with a thud. "Once upon a time…" he starts.

"Never," she retaliates. And she rolls her eyes for emphasis before replacing her glasses. She and Bobbie must have read the same page in the *Secret Handbook of Long Island Rules*, which states that you should never mistake sunglasses for eye shields. They are, first and foremost, for effect.

She's halfway into the room before she takes a look around.

And then she gets really, really quiet. My mother being quiet can mean only one of two things in this situation. Either she's having a heart attack or she's trying to decide if she's been in this house before.

And from the red creeping up her neck, I'd guess her heart is beating just fine. A little fast, but fine.

She glances out the back door once again, only this time she isn't looking at Mark's washboard abs, or my father, holding the end of a board for him.

"What in God's name is he doing to that wall?" she asks.

Is that a quiver I detect in her voice, or is it my imagination?

Casually, as if I'm not hanging on her response, I tell my parents about how the wall obstructs the view, and how we are tearing it down.

My mother fans herself.

"Do you want to sit down, Mom?" I ask her solicitously. *In a confessional, perhaps?*

She glares at me, then looks around the room. "Where's all the furniture?" She fumbles through her purse looking, no doubt, for her cigarettes, even though she knows I won't let her light up in the house.

I tell her I'm working on the furniture, though now I have to wonder if, before I gave the couch away, I should have checked the cushions for bullet holes, or perhaps condoms. Oh, wait. My brother, David, just may be a testament to the fact that there were no condoms, right?

"So what do you see here, Mom?" I ask, shaking my head at her to indicate she'd better not light up, and I throw out more bait to catch her with. "Early American, maybe?"

She looks at me like I've got two heads. "I see Bermuda," she says, putting the unlit cigarette in her mouth and talking around it. "Elbow Beach. I see wide striped canvas in white and beige...."

"Touches of pale turquoise and shell pink," I can't help adding, because I'm more decorator than detective.

"Beige marble floors," she says, her eyes closed as she imagines—maybe the floor, maybe taking a drag.

"Too formal," I say. "Bleached pine."

She smiles. "Probably the way it should have been," she says softly, going to stand by the door so that she can light her cigarette and keep it outside.

We are both quiet while she enjoys her first few puffs. Finally I say, "You've been here before, haven't you?"

"Of course," she answers, waving both her smoke and my question away with her hand. "Everyone's been to the Hamptons. We used to come out here when you were little, remember? Before Markie..." And with that, her voice drifts off.

Okay, here we go. This is going to sound terrible, but I'm convinced that her bringing up Markie is nothing more than subterfuge. Not that my little brother didn't really drown, and not that it didn't break my mother's heart and crack her psyche so badly that she ended up in South Winds Psychiatric Center for months afterward. I don't doubt for a second it was a real blow.

But it was more than thirty-five years ago. Now, whenever my mother wants to change the subject, or have people feel sorry for her, or if she wants to get away with murder, she dredges up poor Markie.

You probably think I'm kidding about the murder part. That's because I haven't mentioned that two years ago at South

Winds she shot Rio in the leg and then calmly walked to the June Bayer Memorial Room where she first ordered in Chinese food and then mumbled about Markie while I blackmailed Rio into not pressing charges.

And today? Someone put love letters, a picture and a gun into the cinder block wall, and when I vaguely refer to her ever having been in this house, what does she do? She trots out Markie.

I didn't tell my mother that the house I was working on belongs to Carmine De'Guiseppe. That wasn't just some oversight, and once she finds out, she'll know it, too. So I can't very well ask her if she remembers this house without opening up Pandora's steamer trunk full of trouble.

Speaking of which… "What's with the bag?" I ask, gesturing toward her LV drag-along, which seems like overkill for a day at the beach. Even for my mother.

"I've decided to stay here and help you," she tells me, still looking distressed as she searches for furniture. "Clearly you need my assistance."

There are many things I need at the moment. Money. Calorie-free ice cream. A phone that can reach Bobbie at sea in Alaska.

But my mother? Here? Not so much.

"Beach houses can go wrong so easily," she tells me, like she's the one with the degree from Parsons. "Too much wicker. Red white and blue. This plastic table, for God's sake."

My head spins around like I need an exorcism and I stare at the table she is pointing at. It's the coffee table I threw out several days ago. *Good*, I think. *Fine. You can't scare me, girly,* because I have a security system that's going to show you carrying that eyesore back in here, you little design-challenged twerp!

I smile at the upper left hand corner of the wall where Rio installed the camera yesterday. Hanging from it, and blocking the lens, is the T-shirt I wore yesterday. I pull over one of the aluminum chairs and yank my T-shirt off the camera.

"What in the world?" my mother asks.

"Security system," I tell her with a shrug.

I should have known that Rio Gallo couldn't solve my problems.

I leave my mother alone with her thoughts, gazing out at the ocean, I mumble something about going to the bathroom, because if I tell her I'm going to call Rio for a better security system, or Drew to tell him that someone's been in the house again…oh, let's just not go there, okay?

After I yell at him for a while, Rio promises a fail-safe solution, and because I've exhausted myself venting, I agree to giving him another chance. And Drew, who picks up on one ring, offers to come out to the cottage, saying he'll stop at the station to fill in the locals. But, he adds, it's an awfully long trip out to the East End, *hint, hint*. Maybe he ought to spend the night.

"My mother's staying over," I tell him. "I doubt all three of us will fit in the bed."

He offers to bring her an air mattress. When I just laugh, he asks whether she knows he's been out here. I choose not to answer, and I can hear from his breathing that he's annoyed. What? I'm supposed to announce to her that I'm seeing Drew again? *That's* a party I don't want to be invited to. Especially since I'd be the main course.

"Look, if you want to deal with her, you just come right on

out and tell her you've got designs on her daughter. Then prepare to duck."

My bedroom door swings open. "Are you talking to me?" Mom asks loudly as she barges in. "I can't hear a word you're saying."

I gesture at the phone in my hand and tell her that's the general idea.

She ignores the hint and stands by the window looking out at the street while Drew tells me he'll alert the local police and be out himself in a few hours.

"Well, give a holler when you're in range," I tell him, and he says he will, and—considering my mother will be here—that he'll wear his Kevlar vest. Just in case.

CHAPTER 9

Saturday night

My mother is strumming her fingernails on the kitchen counter expecting that it will make dinner appear, and I am fabricating an excuse to get out of the house because Rio is on his way over.

Some things never change. Fourteen years ago I could have uttered the same sentence and felt just as desperate.

When the doorbell rings I jump like she's caught us in the back of Rio's pickup. Again.

"*Oy vez mear,*" my mother groans. "Which one of your mistakes is that?"

Actually, it's a good question, but I suggest she's just testy because she's hungry. "Why don't you look through the phone book for a place that delivers while I get the door?"

I toss the local Yellow Pages in her general direction and hurry to the door—faster, I hope, than she can follow me. I open the door just far enough to sneak out and shut it behind me. Rio is on my front step, holding a teddy bear out to me.

"Brilliant," I say sarcastically. "And now anyone watching knows—"

Rio gives me a peck on the cheek and I step back so fast I almost lose my balance. He steadies me, and as he does, I feel him slip something into my back pocket. It could be just his hand—in which case the maneuver will cost him a few fingers. "Smallest wireless microcam on the market," he whispers in my ear. "You put it in a bag of chips or loaf of bread or something."

I'm backed up against the door, and Rio is leaning against me. So, when my mother opens the door, which of course, she does, we both nearly land in her lap.

"Tell me I'm not seeing what I'm seeing," she says. She continues, getting louder and louder with each plea. "Tell me I've taken the wrong pills. That I've lost it this time... Tell me where a damn gun is when I really need it!"

"Rio was just—" I start.

"Hey, June. I was just coming out to check on—" he tries. My mother ignores us both and talks to the clouds.

"Tell me I'm hearing voices," she says, her voice still louder. "Tell me I'm dreaming."

"Tell her to shut up," someone calls from somewhere down the block, followed by gales of laughter.

I push us all into the house, telling her that Rio was just bringing over Alyssa's teddy bear for me to mail up to her. I produce the bear, and get rid of Rio as quickly as I can.

You know, once upon a time, a night like this would be a dream come true. Two dates on the same Saturday night. Of course, the dream wouldn't involve sitting around with my mother, trying to trap an intruder, or having to thank my ex-husband for the use of a wireless microcam.

But seeing the guy calling on my cell phone? Oh, yeah.

"E.T.A.," Detective Scoones says sexily in my ear. "Ten minutes."

"I'm sorry. What did you say happened to the delivery boy?" I say, shaking my head and raising my shoulders at my mother. "Oh, that's too bad. Well, okay. Fine. I guess I'll have to pick up the pizza myself. Yes. Okay. I'll be there in ten minutes."

I hang up, picturing Drew looking at his phone and wearing that smirk he reserves strictly for my dealings with my mother.

When Mom grabs her handbag to accompany me, I remind her that I'm expecting a delivery and that someone has to be here to receive it.

"What could possibly be so important?" she asks me.

I'd love to tell her that a plastic surgeon is coming over to give me an estimate, but I know she'd give up eating and make me stay. Instead I tell her she's waiting for an incredibly handsome man who is bringing a spy camera to me.

"Very funny."

When you think about it, it is. The part about the incredibly handsome man and the spy camera is true. I'm just a little off with the time.

Grabbing a sweater and my keys and running faster than she can keep up with me, I get in my car and drive to the end of the block to wait for Drew.

When he finally shows up, I switch cars, feeling like a character from a spy novel, or yet another of those old movies I watch. I tell him about the microcam and when he asks to see it, I have to squirm and contort to try to get it out of my back pocket in a bucket seat. It's not easy, and Drew is clearly enjoying the show. Eventually he reaches around me, insinuating his hand into my pocket and slipping out the camera with a promise to put it back there when he's done looking at it.

He confirms that it is state-of-the-art, reluctantly seconds Rio's suggestion for its placement, and asks if I've seen any trace of the local police. When I say they haven't shown up, he says they were told to be discreet and not alarm my mother.

I don't know how he really put it to them, but he got across the idea that they should keep an eye on the house without letting the raving lunatics inside know they were there.

Hey, works for me.

"Funny, sitting here in a car kind of hiding from your mother," he says after a while. "Reminds me of being in high school. There was this girl, Lucianne Ashly, and we'd park down the block from her house so her mother wouldn't see me slip my hand under her sweater." He demonstrates deftly. "Like this."

"And did she swat your hand away, like a good girl?" I ask, having no inclination myself to do so, which probably means I'm not the good girl I used to be.

"Not old Lucianne," he assures me. "In fact…"

And that is how we come to steam up the windows pretty completely before I reluctantly lift my head and announce it's time I ought to be heading back.

Drew cracks open the window and accuses me of being a tease, just like old Lucianne.

"Maybe," I tell him. "But all these years later you still remember her name. She must have done something right."

He leans back against his seat, eyes closed, like he's remembering.

Or maybe comparing.

"Teddi, I—" he begins, but a tap on the window interrupts him. I think I see relief on his face.

I know I'm glad whoever it is didn't stroll over and knock a few minutes earlier.

He gives me a second to straighten my clothes and then opens his door and steps out. A minute later I get out on my side to see what's going on. He's talking to a uniformed cop who gives me the once-over before Drew moves to somewhat block his view.

"Old boyfriend, perhaps?" the cop suggests.

Drew shakes his head and tells him we're pretty sure it's a young woman, and that our best guess is she's a runaway who's been living in the house and wants to go on doing so.

The cop agrees to keep an eye peeled, and I get back into my own car to return to my mother.

I find her finishing up her half of the pizza and complaining that they showed up just after I left.

"Just crossed wires, I guess," I say with a shrug while she studies me.

"You look a little flushed," she says suspiciously and I tell her I just rushed to get back so she wouldn't be alone in case…and I let my voice drift off.

It's going to be a long night, I fear, as I do the dishes while she gets ready for bed. It's an elaborate ritual of creams and potions and lotions that ends—mercifully for me—with the swallowing of a handful of pills including a Valium, which she says she needs to sleep.

In an attempt to steal five minutes for myself, I set her up in the living room with some decorating magazines and ask her to fold down the pages she thinks I ought to take a look at.

While she narrates what's wrong with the magazine, the rooms they are showing and every room I've ever decorated, I manage to put the microcam into a bag of chips on the bar before going off to change the linens in the bedroom for her.

And Mark calls and I tell him I'm fine. And Rio calls and I tell him the camera is in a bag of corn chips and no, I didn't forget to be sure there's a hole where the lens is. And Drew calls and tells me to take off my shirt.

"What?"

"I'm outside," he says. "Staked out across the street. I'm bored. Give me something to look at, sweetcakes."

I look out my bedroom window. There's Drew's car, but no one appears to be in it.

"Come on, come on. Give a guy a break."

I pull up the front of my T-shirt for a second. Drew says something about my being a tease and I realize he really can see me. He begins to hum that *Stripper* music.

And I don't know what gets into me, but I gyrate a tiny bit and then pull my shirt off over my head. Maybe it's the knowledge that this man doesn't have to be sitting outside my house in the middle of the night.

And that he is.

Or maybe it's because I just wanna.

"Go, baby," he tells me.

I pull the sheets off the bed, knowing he's watching me, and knowing he's probably thinking it's too bad I don't have a little maid's uniform on.

I'm thinking it's too bad I don't have a little maid.

When I put the phone to my ear, Drew gives me a few

more bars from *The Stripper* and then encourages me to slip out of my jeans.

"Do you usually get an eyeful on a stakeout?" I ask him.

"Uh-huh," he says. "Only the woman's usually four foot eight and weighs three hundred pounds and knows I'm out there."

I can't help laughing.

"Is your mother asleep yet?" he asks, and I say I'll go check.

She's snoring on the chaise in the living room, so I go back into my room and shut the door behind me. Opening the window, I motion to Drew, who gets out of his car, looks both ways, and beelines to my window.

"I'm thinking you could keep a closer eye on the situation from in here," I say. In a heartbeat he's in my room. And he manages it gracefully, too.

And a minute later we're in bed. And not too long after that he's stroking my back and telling me that life with me sure would be interesting.

It stops my breath in my throat. When I catch it, I tell him it's probably time for him to leave. I've got to move my mother into bed or I'll hear all day tomorrow about her stiff neck. And I've got work in the morning that's got to be done. And he knows I'm babbling.

And that I do that when I'm scared.

I think I see surprise in his eyes.

But it could be hurt.

CHAPTER 10

Early Sunday morning

Clutching a light jacket in one hand, Drew slips back out the way he came in. And I throw on a ratty old robe and head for the living room to wake up my mother.

Only I don't have to wake her up because a bullhorn shouting outside the house does it for me.

"Get down on the ground and spread 'em," a deep voice yells, and flashing lights turn the cottage into an arcade.

My mother groggily comes awake and clutches at my arm, asking what I've done now and urging me to give myself up.

I peel her off me and go to the front window. Spread-eagle on what passes for the lawn is Drew Scoones, swearing a blue streak while a uniform pats him down.

If my mother wasn't nestled up against my back watching over my shoulder—not to mention breathing down my neck— this would actually be funny.

The police don't seem to find it so, especially when they discover Drew's gun, and it isn't until he gets them to open his wallet and see his shield that they let him take his face out of the broken shells and gravel.

I insist that my mother stay in the house and go outside to explain the situation away. The police don't really listen. Maybe because my mother has come out on my heels and is shouting that they should arrest Drew and throw away the key.

"He's a stalker," she accuses. "He's been stalking my daughter for over a year. It's not bad enough she's a divorced woman with three children. But she has a police stalker. Who's going to be interested in a woman like that?"

Drew orders my mother inside. Good joke. He tells the police that he and I are *friends*. There's that word again. It's almost enough for me to just let him explain his own way out of this.

They ask him why he was climbing out of my window.

"Out?" my mother asks. "*Out* of her window?"

She glares at me. I smile back innocently.

Drew points with his chin at my mother. "Why do you think?" he asks the cop, who snickers in response.

"There were reports of an intruder," the cop tells me, pretty much ignoring Drew. Ah, the poetic justice of it all. Drew Scones on the hot seat. I have to admit, I love it.

"I made that report," Drew says sharply. "Call your precinct, for Christ's sake."

"He's not an intruder," I assure the cops.

"Well, he's not an invited guest," my mother adds.

"I told you I was going in," Drew says to the cop who is standing just a little too close to him. The cop assures Drew it wasn't him. Change of shift, failure of communication, and then, again, "Why'd you say you were climbing out this woman's window?"

"My mother was asleep in the living room," I say, pulling my robe more tightly around me. "We didn't want to disturb her."

While my mother humphs, the cop sarcastically says, "How considerate," and implies that the drama is now over.

That is, the police drama. He should only know what Drew and I are facing as we accompany my mother into the house.

For a moment I sense a wave of sympathy from Drew that nearly knocks me off my feet.

Is it maybe, for just a second, he got to see what it feels like to be misunderstood, to be simply in the wrong place at the wrong time doing something that might appear to be the wrong thing…in other words, to be me.

CHAPTER 11

Sunday morning

I sneak out of bed, leaving my mother still sleeping. When she finally wakes up, she will swear that she hasn't slept a wink all night, and I will sympathize. In the meantime, I creep out to the kitchen to check whether the self-contained microcamcorder Rio gave me has captured anything on tape.

I can see that Drew's car is gone from in front of the house, and after last night, I'm glad I didn't put the recorder in the bedroom.

The counter on the camcorder shows that it picked up something, and I hook it up to my laptop with the same wires Rio gave me for the other minicams, running the video through my media player. I click on various icons until it seems willing to reveal its secrets.

Finally, I see a dark-haired girl of maybe nineteen or twenty dart across the screen and stop dead in her tracks, most likely when she found Mom asleep on the chaise. She grabs two of my decorating magazines and runs back out.

Somehow I rather doubt she's planning on redecorating the garage.

So now, on the one hand, it's creepy to imagine someone here in the house, possibly while Drew and I were…

But, on the other hand, it's kind of reassuring to see that she's just a kid—probably wishing this house were her own, especially since before I showed up, it pretty much was.

"Who's that?"

You know, for a woman as old as my mother is, she sure can creep silently, and she startles me, which is exactly what she intended.

I tell her I don't know who the girl is, but I'm pretty sure she's been in the cottage a few times before. "That's the intruder they mistook Drew for last night."

My mother says that as far as she's concerned Drew Scoones is a lot more dangerous an intruder than the young woman on my computer. And she wants to know how the picture has come to be on my computer, anyway. I tell her that after she fell asleep last night the security guy came and brought me a microcam.

She tells me she wasn't asleep and he wasn't that cute.

Of course, I can't tell her she's lying without admitting I am, too.

"Fine," I say. *End of conversation, let's just drop it, game over.* I grab a cup of my own coffee, despite my mother's warning that it's weak, and head for the showers.

There's a funky smell in here, but then, it is a bathroom. Still…

I reach in beyond the shower curtain and turn on the water. A horrible noise comes from behind the curtain and I am afraid to look. I don't have to, because out comes a wet, angry skunk, which I wouldn't have to see to know was there, if you get my drift. I've gotten the skunk's drift.

I scream, not because I'm so scared, but because I'm so startled. The skunk bares its teeth.

Okay, now I'm scared. And the smell is overwhelming, noxious. My head begins to swim.

I sidle past it and open the window, gasping for fresh air before I rush back to the door, flattening myself against it.

"Go out," I tell the black-and-white ball of stench. "Come on. Out the window."

It makes a move toward me. I stamp at it. It stamps back.

My mother shouts from the other side of the door. "Are you sick?" she asks me. "What's that terrible smell?"

I try, as calmly as possible, to tell her that I'm trapped in the bathroom with a skunk. An angry, wet, smelly, fearless skunk.

"Don't come out," she tells me. "It'll come with you and be loose in the house."

Gagging, I tell her my plan is to catch the skunk in a towel and throw it out the window, which is only a few feet off the ground. She, in response, tells me that skunks can be rabid and it will bite me and I will have to have rabies shots and then die.

Catching the skunk in a towel no longer sounds like a viable option.

"We should call someone," she says, and I agree while retching. I tell her that I'm coming out of the bathroom, that I'll quickly shut the door behind me, and call an exterminator. The skunk does not appear to like that idea and to prove it, attempts to bite the end of my flip-flop, forcing my plan into fast forward.

I turn around and try to open the door. The knob comes off in my hand.

The skunk has attached itself to the hem of my robe and is making threatening noises.

I put the toilet seat down and climb up on it. The skunk hangs there for a second, then finds its footing with its back legs. I let it have my robe.

"Call someone," I shout to my mother, standing naked on the top of the toilet. She tells me that it smells too bad in the house and she's going out. I've been holding my breath until I must be blue, and she's telling me this like I haven't noticed.

"Listen to me," I say. "Under the mattress in my bedroom is a gun. Get it and my phone, go around the outside of the house and throw them in the window to me."

I hear nothing.

"Mom?"

Just when I am convinced I am going to be found naked and dead in this stinking bathroom, my mother shows up at the window.

"And you don't like the smell of my cigarettes?" she asks me. "Here." She drops the gun and my phone into the bathroom. My phone hits the tile floor and splits into several pieces, one of which the skunk claims as his own.

The gun is just out of reach. I jump down emphatically, hoping to scare the skunk into the corner and grab the gun. I am back up on the toilet taking aim when I realize that I can't kill an animal. I'm two spare ribs away from becoming a vegetarian, after all.

"Okay," I say to the skunk. "I'm going to shoot this gun right next to you and you are going to get so scared that you are going to climb out the window—you got that?" I ask it.

It almost nods.

"Now don't move," I tell it, gasp in some putrid air and hold my breath again.

I take aim, close one eye, and squeeze the trigger. I think I'm actually praying that there are no bullets in the gun, but clearly there is one because I hit the water pipe and water is shooting everywhere.

Not a full minute later there is a policeman outside the bathroom door and another at the window. Through the water spray I can see that the one at the window has his gun drawn.

You know what he can see.

"Get me out of here," I yell at him as his partner bursts through the door.

"Pew!" the policewoman who has broken down the door says, rubbing her shoulder before noticing that I am naked and standing on the toilet, neither of which last long as I go lunging from the room, grab up a blanket from my bedroom and go running out the front door and straight into Drew's arms.

While I tell him about the skunk, like the stench didn't make the situation self-evident, a policewoman—whose tag might read Olivia McKenna, but who I know is really Supergirl because who else would go back into a skenky skunk house—brings out my robe. I can so see Drew wants to laugh, but sucking in air makes all of us gag, so he's stuck with just shaking his head at me. It almost looks like sympathy as he helps me slip into my robe without giving a show to the several neighbors who have come out of their houses to check out the smell.

Drew settles me in his car—windows up, air-conditioning on, stench still there—maybe it's me at this point—and goes into the house. People stare at me angrily and point, like it's my fault there was a skunk in my bathroom, and I stare back because I have nothing to apologize for.

That is, until the people with the PETA signs show up protesting the shooting of skunks. With the air still reeking, they don't get much sympathy. Their noisy presence, however, appears to give Carmine's neighbors one more reason to hate me.

A few minutes later Drew comes out with my purse, some clothes, my mother's suitcase, and assurances.

"All the windows are open. You were damn lucky it sprayed in the shower and not at you, you know. You're going to need a plumber, but I've turned off the water at the main for now."

He wets his handkerchief with bottled water and hands it to me.

"Cheer up," he tells me, dabbing at the tears running from my eyes because of the smell. "This wasn't your fault."

It's the first time he's ever said that to me. Maybe the first time *anyone's* said that to me. My body reacts like it's been jolted with electricity.

He pushes the hair out of my eyes and adjusts the front of my robe, and I'm just beginning to calm down when he looks around at the crowd. "Where's your mother, anyway?"

CHAPTER 12

Two days later, we've moved out of the motel and back into the cottage—which now smells only faintly of skunk because there was so little for the odor to cling to—my mother and I wake in the new king-size bed that fills the bedroom from wall to wall.

We pad into the kitchen together, she angry with me for breathing—or maybe for suggesting she go home. I suppose that could be it. I'm not thrilled with her, either, since she insisted we share a room at the motel so that you-know-who couldn't make a midnight visit.

Anyway, I offer to make coffee, which Mom criticizes but expects, and when someone knocks on the front door, we're both still in our pajamas.

"Teddi?" a familiar voice I wasn't expecting calls out through the front door. "You there?"

I tell my mother to go get dressed and we argue long enough for my caller to walk around to the glass door and peek in, his hands cupped around his face. Even pressed up against the glass, my mother recognizes him and goes running down the hall with her hands covering her unmade-up face.

"What's *he* doing here?" she asks from the bedroom while I

slide open the glass door and let in my client and the owner of the house we're sleeping in, Carmine De'Guiseppe.

His face is positively glowing. "Was that your mother I saw?" he asks me, hope so bright it's nearly blinding.

Before I can lie and tell him he's mistaken, my mother calls out from the bedroom. "Bring my makeup case in here," she says.

And Carmine beams.

"She wouldn't let my dog see her without makeup, so don't go thinking she wants to look good for you," I tell him over my shoulder as I get my mother's train case from the bathroom and place it on the floor outside the bedroom door.

"I'll be back in a few minutes," he yells to her. Then to me he says, "I'll go get some pastries from the Golden Pear and be back before she's done fixing her face."

He could take until Tuesday and I'm willing to bet she still wouldn't be done until ten minutes after he returns.

Three-quarters of an hour later, Carmine and my mother are begging me to give them some time alone. Carmine assures me they are just going to talk. My mother seems vaguely disappointed by his promise. She announces that she's going home in the afternoon anyway, so what can a few minutes of talking hurt?

And I'm so happy that she's leaving today that I grudgingly go off for a walk with my cell phone, leaving them to "talk."

Drew calls while I'm pacing in front of the house and says it's a gorgeous day. He tells me there's not a cloud in the sky. "A great day for a barbecue on the beach," he adds.

If he's fishing for an invitation, he's going to have to be more direct.

"I'll bring the steaks," he finally says. "And the beer and Pepsi."

At this point it's hard to work up much enthusiasm. "Whatever," is about the best I can do. Apparently, it's good enough for Drew, who says he'll be over later.

After half an hour of pacing in the sun, I decide this is ridiculous, and I return to the cottage to confront my mother and her suiter. Only they aren't there. Just a couple of empty glasses and the bag of chips on the counter, just the way I left it, with the microcam replaced inside.

I know that technically, I shouldn't even look. But, come on. If you found a gun in a wall, knew that your mother and some man had a history, knew that they probably discussed that history and you could actually be that fly on the wall you're always wishing you could be…

No? You *really* wouldn't look?

Well, then you're a better man than I am, because I hit that Play icon faster than you can say Carmine De'Guiseppe— which isn't really all that fast.

I see Carmine try to take my mother's hand. I watch her turn her head away.

"You remember this place?" he asks her.

"It's too long ago," she says. "Too much water under the bridge."

"This couldn't be, maybe, a second chance?" he asks.

I hold my breath waiting for my mother's response. She says nothing, as though she is waiting to be convinced, to be wooed.

"It was good here," he says. "Remember the fires on the beach? The fires in my heart…in my loins?"

"Fires die," my mother says. "They burn themselves out and

sometimes they reduce everything to ashes and just blow away like they were never there."

Who is this woman? My mother has never sounded this poetic.

"You should have told me about the baby," Carmine says. His voice is tinged with anger. "I had a right to know."

My mother doesn't respond well to anyone's anger but her own. In fact, no one else is entitled to any. To prove this, she gives Carmine the *stare*.

But it doesn't stop him. "You had no right—" he starts, but my mother cuts him off.

She says that she came to tell him. "Here. In our special place." Only when she got here, she found the gun and the proof that he was going into the *family business* despite his promises.

When he begins to deny it, she stops him.

"And the police came. I was standing with your baby in my belly, and your gun in my hand, and the police were at the door."

Carmine covers his mouth with his hand. "It wasn't my—"

My mother continues, but her back is to Carmine so that she doesn't have to look at him. "I didn't know what to do. Raymond was building the wall, but he was gone for the day, so I stuck the gun deep into one of the cinder blocks. And then I put in my letters to you and the picture from that day you proposed. I couldn't just destroy all that, but I knew it was over between us. And I walked down the beach, knowing I couldn't marry you, couldn't live this life. Just like I said in my note."

Now she turns to face him and all I can see is the sagging of her shoulders and the heavy breathing that fills her back and seems to deflate when she speaks.

"And then I went to Marty, and I told him, because I knew

that he loved me then and would always love me. And I told him the truth."

Carmine asks if my father knew about the baby and my mother nods and says that he asked her to marry him, *begged* her to marry him, knowing she was carrying Carmine's child. "He promised that, as far as he was concerned, the child would be his own in every way. And he kept that promise."

I can see Carmine's face, watch him bite at the edge of his lip, as he listens without interrupting. Finally, when my mother is silent, he says that her assumptions were all wrong. The gun, he contends, was planted by enemies of the family. "My father got wind of the setup and sent me away. If I'd been on this side of the ocean, do you think I'd have let you get away from me?" he asks.

I am embarrassed to be a witness to all of this, and yet I can't pull my eyes away, can't turn the computer off, can't give them the privacy the moment deserves.

I watch, transfixed, as my mother tells the man she once loved—maybe still loves—that it is too late and it doesn't matter. He chose the kind of life he wanted to lead, and she would never have any part of it.

Carmine tells her that his life isn't what it seems. "Do you really think for one minute that the cop who's got the hots for your daughter would let me within ten miles of her if I was what you think I am?"

"Detective *Spoonbrain* is supposed to be your proof of a straight life?" she asks. I notice she is looking directly at the bag of chips in which I've hidden the camera.

Now, it could be that she's just hungry. But I'm thinking not. "Too late. Forty years too late."

I miss what Carmine says, and I try to back the recording up slightly. He is begging her to let him into her life. "As a friend, then. Just an old family friend."

My mother takes her sweet time with a response. I think it is for dramatic effect, but I'm not sure for whose benefit— Carmine's or mine. And then she tells us both that all these years have proven one thing. That she made the right choice. She's happy. She has respect, social standing. She's important at the temple. She likes her life and she's grown to love Marty. As much, she suspects, as she's capable of loving anyone.

I hear my mother's and Carmine's voices before I see them at the back door. Since my eyes are glued to the laptop, that's not surprising. I slam the lid down on the computer as Carmine slides open the glass door and allows my mother to enter. She gets a smug look on her face when she sees me standing by the bar.

Just as Carmine is about to follow her in, the girl I've caught on the microcam appears from nowhere and tells him she knows what he is up to. And that he should be ashamed of himself.

I have to admit he looks completely baffled. He squints at her in the strong sunlight, putting his hand up to shield his eyes. "Terri?" he says, as if he's trying to place her but isn't quite sure she's who he thinks she is.

"That woman is young enough to be your daughter," she says, pointing at me.

None of us says that I almost was.

Then she tells him that he's making a fool out of himself, which, she says, he deserves to be made, but still…

She points at me. "Your little *goomah* here—" she starts.

"His *what?*" I demand, but she's on a roll. And she's not about to stop to respond to Carmine's *goomah*.

"You think she's just sitting on her fat ass when you're not here?" she asks, storming past Carmine and into the cottage.

I take exception to my butt being called fat, and try to catch a reflection of it in the glass doors while she rants on about how I've got men coming and going.

Not bad for a fat woman, huh?

"The security guy can't keep his hands off her," she says, and my mother and Carmine stare at me, shocked.

"Rio," I say by way of explanation. Of course, that doesn't really help my case.

"And the carpenter—" she says, and rolls her eyes.

I say something about Mark working for me and since I don't know why I'm defending myself to this trespasser, I just throw up my hands to indicate that I couldn't care less what she thinks.

"And does the guy in the Mazda RX7 work for you, too?" she asks. "Because if what you were doing that night in the rain was paying him, I think that's illegal."

"What is *really* illegal—" I start to tell her, but my mother doesn't let me finish.

"A Mazda RX7? For God's sake, Teddi. You told me the other night was the first time—" my mother says. "If I've told you once—"

The girl looks at me with a certain amount of sympathy. I guess she's heard the same speech herself. "Blah. Blah, blah," she tells my mother. "What do you have to do with all this, anyway?" I've never heard anyone talk to my mother that way, and I have to admire the kid, even though I know she is about to be demolished.

My mother assures her she'll get to her when she's done with me.

"You've been trysting with that worthless excuse for—" she starts.

"No, I wasn't. Rio was just dropping off—" I start, when who should waltz in the front door, but my father?

"What about Rio?" he asks. We all ignore him.

"I meant Detective Spoonbreath," my mother says.

"Just how many men are you screwing around with anyway?" the girl asks. I think she's actually impressed.

"You watch your mouth, young lady!" Carmine says, while at the same time my father takes exception to my virtue being impugned.

"My daughter," he begins, but the young lady stops him in his tracks.

The girl is a force to be reckoned with. I'll give her that.

"Your daughter?" she says. "See, Uncle Carmine? She's young enough to be—"

"Uncle Carmine?" I say. My mother echoes me.

"I thought you wanted to spend time with *Teddi*," my father says to my mother, oblivious to any other drama being played out. "But no, this was all a ruse to see your old beau, wasn't it?" He gestures toward Carmine, whose face is somewhere between red and purple.

Terri scoffs at the idea of my mother and Carmine. "The old lady? He hasn't so much as held that one's hand. But her," she says, gesturing at me. "That one he's all over."

We are all shouting so loudly at this point that a whole party could saunter in and we'd never notice.

Which, wouldn't you know it, apparently happens, because when I turn around to yell at my father—who is accusing my mother of lying about seeing Carmine while she is yelling at Terri for calling her old—Drew is standing just inside the front door. And behind him are Hal and Hallie.

"That's the guy," Terri says. "The one she was in the car with, giving him—"

Hal puts two fingers in his mouth and whistles so sharply that we all put our hands up to our ears.

And we all shush.

In the quiet I say softly to my father, "Mom didn't plan to meet Carmine here. She didn't know this place was his. Did you, Mom?" I ask, expecting her to say that, of course, she didn't.

She says nothing.

"Mom?"

She looks at my father. "Maybe I knew," she says with a slight shrug of her shoulders.

"You're interested in *her*?" Terri asks Carmine, pointing at my mother.

Carmine avoids answering by telling Terri how worried her father has been about the girl.

"And *you're* interested in her, too?" Terri asks my father. Her tone is now incredulous.

My father denies being interested in my mother. "No, I'm not interested in her," he says. "I'm married to her."

I see Hallie hide a smile.

Terri is still trying to get it all straight. She asks Drew who he is interested in. He says he's interested in throwing some steaks on the grill.

"Nice save," I say.

"Nice try," my mother says.

"Nice steaks," Hal says.

"What about you?" Terri asks Hal. "Where do you fit in here?"

Hal leans against a wall. "Well," he says, and he's got just enough smirk going to make me want to smack him. Of course, when it comes to Hal, that's any smirk at all. In fact, even sans smirk… "Scoones here thought I got the wrong impression the other day, and if I just came by again I'd see the whole family wasn't whacko."

I smile at Drew. It's nice that he thinks I'm not a whack job.

Actually, he looks less sure about that now that he's here, but he puts his arm around me nonetheless, almost as if to stake some sort of claim.

"So this is your niece," I ask Carmine, eyeing Terri with contempt while she squirms. "Nice. Putting the furniture I threw out back. Moving things around. Covering the security camera with my shirt."

She says she was only protecting her great-uncle. "I thought you were two-timing him," she says with that teenage whine that is supposed to justify any wrongdoing. "I mean, you could have given him AIDS or something."

I'm so furious that I almost miss her suddenly fussing with her hair and straightening her shirt while her eyes go right over my shoulder. I turn my head to see what she's looking at and see Mark sauntering down the block.

After he's passed the cars of all the people surrounding me,

I introduce him to the owner of the bikini. Drew seems delighted that Mark's gaze is locked on Terri and not me.

People begin to see the humor of the situation—imagine Carmine interested in me, or me interested in Rio, or Mark, or…I look at Drew. He is smiling—not smirking, but smiling. My mother learns that Terri is motherless and moves in for the kill. Terri doesn't seem to object to my mother's unsolicited advice, though I notice my mother's warnings don't stop her from shooting furtive glances Mark's way.

So rather than break the mood, I invite everyone to stay for a barbecue on the beach, offering to go get some lobsters or steaks and corn on the cob.

Hal says he has some beach chairs in the car, adding something snide about figuring I wouldn't have anywhere for him to sit, and my father and Carmine argue about who should light the grill and nearly come to blows until Terri suggests that Mark do it and the men agree.

Drew says he'll go get the food, and asks me to come with him, reaching out his hand to me.

I take it and we head toward his car. "Teddi, I…" he starts, and I feel something momentous coming. Either he wants to ditch me or take this relationship to the next step.

I'm not so sure which one scares me more, so I stop in my tracks and put up my finger.

"You go ahead," I say, waving him toward the car. "I just remembered something."

He looks at me, studying me, trying to read what's on my mind, but even I'm not so sure. Can I really tell him that I'm remembering how hard I had to fight for my independence, my confidence, my sense of self? And how fragile all of that still is? How at risk? And how I'm just not ready to give any of that up, at least not right now?

"We need to talk, Teddi," he tells me.

And I revert to my movie archives and tell him sure, "Tomorrow."

After all, as Scarlett said, tomorrow is another day.

* * * * *

Just what will tomorrow bring? Find out in Stevi Mittman's next
Life On Long Island Can Be Murder adventure,
Whose Number is Up Next, Anyway?
Coming in August, 2007, from Harlequin NEXT.

SUMMERTIME BLUES

KATE AUSTIN

From the Author

Dear Reader,

I can't tell you how much I love the aquarium—it's one of my favorite places in the whole world. And it's not just my hometown aquarium. It's every single one of them.

Last summer I spent a lot of time in aquariums—in Atlanta and in Vancouver—doing research for this book. I watched fish, stood mesmerized in front of the jellyfish, dreamed of the Amazon jungle, talked to volunteers, drooled over the goodies in the gift shops. It was a perfect way to spend the summer and a perfect way to get ready to write Ardella's story. What happens to Ardella—finding the thing she wanted to do and the person she wanted to be—in one magical summer afternoon at the aquarium is a miracle. I envy her—it took me twenty years longer than Ardella's thirteen to find out what I wanted to do with my life. I envy her the certainty of that knowledge, but most of all, I envy her all those hours at the aquarium.

I hope you enjoy her story and I hope, more than anything, that it sends you off to the aquarium for an afternoon. You'll love it. I promise.

Have a wonderful summer—and don't forget the fish!

Kate

For Mary Louise and Susan—who happily spent time at the aquarium with me.

CHAPTER 1

Weedy scorpionfish (Rhinopias aphanes):
Disguises itself as seaweed and
waves in the current, waiting
to snag any unsuspecting prey
that might float by

Ardella wondered if brides or mothers-to-be felt this unbearable combination of sheer, unadulterated panic and mindblowing joy. And if they did, she couldn't understand how so many of them managed to make it down the aisle or give birth without bolting.

She could barely walk. Her legs felt like limp spaghetti and her ankles and knees didn't want to support her. If she'd been behind the wheel of a car, she'd have killed someone. Nothing, not a single thing over the difficult years, had made Ardella feel this way.

She was a coper—she coped with illness, with bureaucracy, without her dreams. She could do anything. Really.

Except maybe not this.

Her heart pounded—a deep, almost painful thumping—in time with her footsteps on the pavement. But all the stresses and strains of the past twenty years vanished in the joy of walking toward the *employee* entrance of the place that had been her true home for as long as she could remember.

The aquarium had saved her sanity—and maybe even her life—and now she was going to work here. She hurried down the path to the door and then stopped when she caught a glimpse of herself in the mirrored windows. She wore the aquarium's royal blue employee shirt with the logo—a white starfish and the name—over her left breast.

It wasn't quite warm enough for her white walking shorts—not in Vancouver at the very beginning of June—but Ardella had worn them anyway.

She'd imagined wearing these exact clothes, imagined herself striding through the back passages of the aquarium, mistress of all she surveyed.

And now here she was.

Starting at the bottom of the heap.

But one day soon Ardella Simpson was going to be a force to be reckoned with. Every single one of those fish, and the mammals for that matter, would listen to her.

Twenty years ago she'd been on her way to a degree in marine biology when her mother got ill. Twenty years of home nursing, of cooking and cleaning and negotiating with health-care providers and Ardella had wondered—sometimes still did wonder—if she might not be too old or too tired to start all over again.

Not that forty was old, she thought. After all, didn't the magazines say that forty was the new thirty and surely thirty wasn't old?

This summer as a volunteer was a test.

She missed her mother, had never once begrudged the time or energy spent caring for her, never regretted giving up her dream, but now it was time to see if it was possible.

She sold the condo to pay their debts and her tuition. She'd packed up her mother's belongings and Ardella was on her way.

She wasn't sure whether she actually felt twenty again but that's what she was aiming for. Lighthearted yet committed to her future. Friendly and open instead of closed off. Willing to take risks.

That was going to be the hardest part of this experiment.

Ardella had spent the last twenty years—through no fault of her own—being extremely risk-averse. But if she wanted to become the woman she'd dreamed of being, she would have to take all kinds of risks. She squared her shoulders, smiled at the woman—in royal blue and white—reflected in the window and pressed the buzzer on the door. She was ready. At least she thought she was ready.

The flight instinct—once again—reared its ugly head, making her heart pound, her palms sweat and her face red. She took a step back from the door. And then another.

"Careful," a voice said behind her. "You're going to step on my brand-new sneakers.

"Not," the voice continued as if musing to herself, "that it really matters. They'll have fish guts and slime all over them within a week. It doesn't matter what detergent I use, and I've used them all, nothing gets that slime out. I don't know why I bother, but I love the look and feel of new sneakers.

"I buy five or six pairs a year. Have to. It's not so hard on your clothes—they wash better. But the shoes? Two months, tops, and then they look like I've worn them for a two-week vacation on the seventh level of hell.

"I'm Marney. Marney Kenner. I've worked here forever. You know, narrate the shows, talk to the kids, make sure they don't fall into the water?"

Ardella, whose flight instinct had been suppressed by the outpouring of unrequested information, simply nodded, then feeling the nod not quite enough, said, "Yes. I've seen you, I think."

She paused for a minute, checking out her heart, palms and face. All normal. Maybe the flight instinct had vanished, maybe she was going to be okay. She still wavered between turning around and heading for the exit or talking to Marney so she could get herself to walk in the door. Ardella chose the latter.

"I'm Ardella Simpson."

"Your first day? I can tell by the look on your face, a lot nervous and a little excited. I remember—" Marney pushed open the door when the red light on the handle turned green "—my first day. I spent almost all of it trying not to puke."

"Have you worked here long?" Ardella felt a bit nauseous herself as she hurried through the back corridors after Marney who never, not even for a moment, stopped talking.

"Ten years this summer. I volunteered during high school and college—my degree's in communications—and just never left. There are lots of us like that. Not many like you, though. Not first timers."

Ardella endured Marney's careful perusal of her.

"You're a little older—" Marney giggled "—than our usual new recruits."

Ardella had to smile back at that carefully judged *little*. She expected she was a whole lot older than the rest of the new kids; she expected that *kids* was the operative word.

"Lunchroom's over there. Showers—not that they help, even with the soap we use, if you're spending your days preparing breakfast, lunch and dinner for our inhabitants. Helps even less if you add cleaning tanks to your repertoire."

"Do you do that?" Ardella leaned forward a little and sniffed. No fishy smell, just soap and shampoo.

"Not anymore. But I used to. My first couple of summers? The only people who'd come near me were the kids who were doing the same job. The only people I talked to those summers were people at the aquarium. I didn't have a date for two whole summers except casual ones with the other volunteers, and those were my prime dating years."

Ardella smiled to herself at the thought of a date. She basically hadn't had a serious one for almost twenty years. A slight exaggeration, maybe, but close to the truth.

She'd had dozens of first dates but as soon as those men found out that she might have to hurry home if her pager went off, she might as well have been gone already.

Years of being on call twenty-four hours a day had put a dent not only in her dating but in her friends. Missing out on them because she smelled like fish seemed like a step forward rather than back.

"I think," Ardella said, taking a risk with her pride, "I'm going to be doing just that. Lowest of the low—cleaning tanks and preparing meals." She smiled, mostly to herself. "Not much different than what I've been doing. Just in a much more beautiful place."

Marney, towing her along behind, had just popped out of the windowless concrete corridors into the office space laid out above the aquarium's great hall.

Ardella stopped in her tracks. She'd been here for her interview but had been too nervous to enjoy the view. Besides, it had been gray and raining all those weeks ago.

Now the sky was the pure, clear blue of a early June day, a few white fluffy clouds adding texture to its beauty. The sun shot sparks off the belugas' pool and the tall cool green cedars in the background added depth.

Home, her heart said. *You're finally home.*

And when one of the belugas surfaced—and soon, Ardella promised herself, she'd know which one it was at first glance—its head tilted as if to say *hello*. Ardella, for only the second time in her life, fell in love.

CHAPTER 2

Jellyfish (Cnidaria Scyphozoa):
Fish-eating animals that
float in the sea. They have soft
bodies and long, stinging, poisonous
tentacles that they use to catch fish.
A jellyfish is 98% water.

The first time had been as a teenager. She'd grown up on the great plains of Saskatchewan—big blue bowl of a sky, winter and summer. The horizon so far away that most days it just vanished into the haze of forever. The prairies had no discretion; they exposed themselves to everyone.

Ardella grew up in a place where the bones of the land were right there to be seen, no mystery, no clothing. Beautiful, yes, and she still missed those crystal-clear nights, something unheard of in this city's clutter of light pollution.

She'd been thirteen when her mother brought her to the coast for a vacation. A summer holiday in Vancouver was a rite of passage in the small towns of the prairies, something to brag about for the following school year, and Ardella had planned to do just that.

They did the usual tourist things—Stanley Park, the ferry over to Vancouver Island, which mostly scared Ardella to death. She'd never imagined so much water all in one place.

They walked down Robson Street, marvelling at the shops and restaurants, but gawking at the number of people in one place, on one street, at one time. They'd picnicked on the beach at English Bay, even swam in the salty cool water, so different from the tiny lake back home.

And then it happened. On the day before they were to leave for home, Ardella fell in love.

"What do you want to do today, Della?" her mother asked. "We can take the gondola up to Grouse Mountain or we can go to the aquarium. Doesn't matter to me."

It didn't matter to Ardella, either, so they flipped a coin and the aquarium won.

Ardella still thought about how odd love was, still pondered the meaning of that coin toss. What if she'd gone to Grouse Mountain instead? Would she have spent all her life pining for something she couldn't define? Or would she have found something else to love?

Her mother never did. She'd married Frank Simpson on her twenty-first birthday. He died ten months later in a stupid accident—that's what her mother always called it.

But Sylvia loved Frank until the day she died, having lived more of her life loving him than not, having spent two years with him and almost sixty without.

Ardella supposed that her ability to sustain love without having its object around came to her naturally. She never did decide whether that was a good or a bad thing.

Yet she would never forget, or regret, that summer day in the July of her thirteenth year.

They drove through Stanley Park—as they'd done every single day of their trip—making goo-goo eyes at the trees, taller than any buildings they'd seen before this visit to the big city. They stopped, as always, to stare at the mountains overwhelming the water. They smiled at the lighthouse, the people on their wobbling bikes, the flowers and the fountain in the lagoon. They laughed at the big old farm horses hitched to a wagon of tourists and stopped to admire the police on their tall bays, the horses as calm and dignified as their riders.

Ardella had no indication that morning that her life was about to change forever, no warning at all. No magpies flying overhead, no black cats crossing her path, no ladders to walk under. They walked from the car park through the zoo to the entrance of the aquarium.

Looking up at the mountains on their way in, she even felt a pang of regret. "Maybe we should go up to Grouse Mountain," she said.

"We're here now, Della. Let's try it for half an hour and if we don't like it, we'll go up the mountain later."

The entrance to the aquarium held no sign of what lay within, it was simply a door with a seller of tickets, like a ticket booth at a movie house, Ardella thought at the time. The entrance to the aquarium was through the gift shop—interesting, maybe, but certainly not memorable.

But then it happened. They turned right out of the entrance hall, walked through a dark corridor into an even darker space and there it was.

Ardella's world.

Backlit tanks of brilliantly colored tropical fish swimming through forests of coral. Octopi clinging to the glass so only their round tentacles were visible. Seahorses standing as still as sentries. Green stickfish hiding among the waving water plants.

She couldn't tear herself away, not even for lunch. Her mother finally left her standing in front of a tank of almost translucent jellyfish, her nose pressed against the glass, mesmerized.

They were the last people to leave the aquarium that day, Ardella's arms piled with every brochure, every pamphlet, every piece of free information they had to offer, along with two books—the cheapest ones—and a souvenir that still sat on her dresser twenty-seven years later.

It was a dried starfish. Not very big, not much wider across than the palm of her hand, and the palest of golds. Even dried, Ardella could feel the texture of it, imagine it clinging to the rocky shore of the Pacific Ocean as it did in its tank.

She spent the next seven years preparing for university, preparing herself to spend a life with her first love.

Well, that life was a little—Ardella laughed at that so she wouldn't cry—delayed, but here she was.

Her first day working at the aquarium. She tried not to think about how her stomach responded to all this excitement, and thanked heaven she'd remembered to buy, and wear, extra-strength deodorant. Not that the smell of her sweat was going to be noticed, not if what Marney had told her was true.

Ardella looked down at her pristine white shorts, socks and runners and shrugged. She'd happily smell like fish for the rest of her life. She'd happily give up dating—she, unlike Marney, wouldn't have the option of dating her fellow newbies—forever.

She didn't care. She was here, looking out over her new world. It felt like a fairy tale, one with a very happy ending.

CHAPTER 3

Arapaima (Arapaima gigas):
Largest scaled freshwater fish in the world.
Newly hatched fish take refuge
inside the adult's mouth.

Ardella had completely forgotten about Marney standing next to her on the balcony, she'd forgotten about everything except her joy at finally being in this place. But she could already tell that Marney wasn't the kind of woman you could forget about for long.

"I'll drop you off at the director's office," Marney said. "She's a sweetheart and one of her favorite things is giving the whole orientation speech and tour. I think there are four or five new people starting today. Half of the summer students are going to be back again from last year but there are a few new ones.

"I'll just leave you here."

And off she went, leaving Ardella in a small waiting room with three babies. Okay, maybe they weren't babies but she'd be surprised if they were more than twenty—any one of them.

"Hi," she said, deciding that this was another test—of her lightheartedness and courage this time. "I'm Ardella."

"Joe," the tall lanky blond boy said. "I'm from Newfoundland."

Ardella smiled. His provenance had been obvious the minute he opened his mouth.

"Terry," the tiny redhead offered. "I'm from here, just over the bridge, really."

"Nick," the dark boy in the corner said. "I'm from Winnipeg."

She smiled at all of them, imagining herself at their age, eager, excited, without a worry or concern. Just a whole summer full of fun to look forward to.

Maybe that's what Ardella should aim for, maybe this could be her vacation—the only one she'd had since—well, since forever.

She thought about that for a while. The trip to the coast when she was thirteen, then the rest of her high school summers working, saving for college. Then her mom got sick and since then? A few weekend trips when her mother was feeling well enough to travel, but never on a plane, never more than a few hours from home. Never far because it was too hard on her mother to be away from her doctors, her safety net, her home.

They'd moved to Vancouver after Ardella finished high school because her brother couldn't bear the cold winters of the prairies. The city had become their home—and the aquarium Ardella's refuge.

So right there and then, as soon as she got the letter telling her she had the job, Ardella decided that this summer would be her gift to herself, a vacation to make up for all the holidays she'd missed. And this was the perfect place for it.

She'd visit the tropics, the Queen Charlottes, the Arctic.

She'd spend time in the jungle with the butterflies and the scarlet ibis and the caiman. She'd see exotic bugs and even more exotic fish.

It was her idea of the perfect vacation.

She thought she'd probably spend most of the next three months smiling and she couldn't wait to get started.

The door to the director's office opened and Ardella, along with the others, stood up to greet the woman who'd interviewed her.

Except that wasn't who appeared from behind the door marked *Denise Allen*.

"Hi," a laughing voice said. "I guess I'm not who you expected to see."

He sounded as if he were used to surprising people and looked as if it didn't matter a bit.

"I'm Greg Angus," he said, "the new co-director. Denise is spending most of the summer on various expeditions so I'll be your guide. And if you need anything at all—" he smiled around the room, his eyes lingering, Ardella thought with a flash of pique, on her "—my door is always open."

"Except this morning." Ardella opened her mouth and out it came, bringing a flush along with it. *That's it*, she thought, *antagonize the boss on your very first day*.

GREG ANGUS LAUGHED. "This isn't my door. I don't have a door." In fact, he wanted to point out to the woman who had to be Ardella Simpson, he'd never had an office door. He'd worked for the aquarium—volunteer and paid—for almost twenty years and he'd never had a door of his own.

Tents, yes. Hatchways, yes. Kayaks and canoes and ice-breakers filled with equipment, but never a door.

But this year he'd been forced into it. The powers-that-be had spoken. "Greg, you've been in the field for twenty years, it's time for you to share some of that expertise with our staff and our visitors."

He'd said no, said it as many different ways as he could think of, but they won. So here he was, shepherding a crew of inexperienced, young—except for Ardella, which was how he'd already begun to think of her—volunteers. Shepherding them through tasks he knew nothing about.

He shook off the unhappiness he felt about being grounded and continued. "I don't close the door or the blinds, either." Would he tell them about why *he* was supervising and not Denise? *Hell*, he thought, *why not?*

"I've been grounded for this summer so I'm borrowing Denise's office for a few months while she's away. And then I'll be back out in the field." He hoped he wasn't lying—to them or to himself.

"I'm nosy and I'm social. I like to know what's going on and I like to talk. To everybody."

GREG ANGUS WAS NOT at all the kind of boss Ardella had expected, not at all who she anticipated spending her summer with. He scared her with his big, booming voice, his sunburned face and eyes—the green of the ocean on an October day—cradled in a network of laugh lines.

He scared her because in some ways he had the face she'd always wanted for herself, a face radiating the confidence and skill she craved.

Denise would have been the perfect boss. She was a woman her age, who would understand Ardella's goals. Greg Angus was going to be much more difficult.

She tried to hide herself at the back of the pack of newbies, hoping he'd give up with his handshakes and his conversations before he got to her. No such luck.

"Ardella Simpson?"

"Yes," she said, stirring up her courage and holding out her shaking hand.

He grasped it, his hand big and warm and callused, its deep brown almost shocking against the winter paleness of hers.

"I'm glad you're here," he whispered. "The others are all so young." The laugh lines around his eyes wrinkled when he grinned at her. "And they're already tiring me out. And the biggest part of my job this summer…"

Ardella closed her eyes, hoping she was wrong about what he was going to say.

"Open your eyes," he said, patting the hand he still held clasped in his, "you don't want to miss anything, not after all these years."

Of course he'd read her résumé and the impassioned letter she'd sent along with it. Of course he knew every boring detail of her life to date. Things couldn't get any worse.

They did.

"The biggest part of my job this summer—" he smiled right into her eyes "—is making sure that all of you work your asses off and learn everything you need to take to school with you.

"Come on," he said, grabbing her hand and towing her—in shock—after him. "It's time to take the tour."

Like Marney, Greg Angus was a talker. Ardella wondered if that was a result of working for too long on the water or in this amazing place, if it was a response to the deep silence of most of the creatures housed here. She wondered if her long silence was about to be broken and if her voice could cope with a sudden influx—or would it be outflux?—of speaking.

The tour took in the public areas—the Great Hall, the outdoor pools. The underground viewing areas, Clownfish Cove, the childrens' section—and then it took in lunch.

One big table, outside on the patio next to the UpStream Café, sandwiches and salads and desserts waiting for them when they arrived.

"You won't get free food again," Greg Angus said, "but they've told me it's a tradition with brand-new volunteers so here." He gestured and swept an overblown bow at the four of them, his eyes once again lingering—once again agitating her—on Ardella.

And then, to anger her even more, he obviously maneuvered the seating so *he* got to sit beside her. She, equally obviously, turned away from him to talk to the others and watch the crowds enjoying the aquarium and the early summer sun.

Greg made certain she was right with him during the whole tour, though Ardella gave him the benefit of the doubt—he only wanted her to hear and see everything and he wasn't so solicitous because she was old. And old she felt with this group. Any one of them could have been a child of hers.

Except Greg, who was her age, maybe a few years younger. Or older. The deep tan and the lines of a man who'd worked outdoors most of his life made his age hard to peg with any accuracy.

The afternoon tour went deeper into the hitherto unseen parts of the aquarium, places Ardella had dreamed about for most of her life. Engineering, maintenance, the feeding stores—all of the nuts and bolts, the *real* life of the aquarium, the places visitors never saw.

The joy of being there, being a part of it, came close to overpowering her. She fought off the sting of tears half a dozen times, ignored the chill accompanying the goose bumps riding her spine.

She kept her eyes firmly on the sights and even more firmly off Greg Angus's face, tempting though it was.

Because she'd spent much of the time since she first saw him wondering how long it would take her to have a face like his. She wanted the deepwater tan, the lines carving his face like a paddle through the sea. She wanted the calmness he wore like a cloak. And, most especially, she wanted the knowledge, the bright sense of competence that shone from his eyes.

She could do without the inability to stop talking, but she wanted everything else.

CHAPTER 4

Giant Pacific Octopus
(Octopus dofleini):
Lives in caves in the rocky reefs
of the north Pacific coast. Comes out
at night to hunt prey of crabs and fishes.

The first real day of her dream job. Ardella again arrived at the door with Marney right behind her and braced herself for the onslaught.

She'd gone home the night before, tired and excited and somehow even more frightened than she'd been before she started the job. But the hours of silence—no radio, no TV, she'd even turned off the phone though the chances of it ringing were slim to none—soothed her enough that here she was. Again.

"How was your first day?" Marney asked but didn't wait for an answer. "I remember that tour. Neither Denise nor Greg were here then so the Old Man took me around. I was the only summer student that year and I'd worshipped him forever. I was scared to death."

"Me, too." Ardella finally got a word in and took advantage

of it. "I've imagined this day for so long and now that it's here, that I'm here? I'm not sure I can do it."

"Of course you can. I did. Hundreds of us since then have. And you've got experience—"

"Age, you mean," Ardella interrupted.

"No," Marney insisted. "I mean experience, life experience. When I got here I knew whatever I did—from cleaning a tank to dropping a bucket of fish on the Old Man's shoes—would change my life forever. Now I know it's not that serious, but I sweated every single decision I made that summer, worried that any move I made would mean life or death to me."

"And it didn't?" Ardella's question was at least half serious.

"Of course not and that's the big advantage you have over the others. You know if you drop a bucket of fish on Greg's feet, it won't change your life forever."

"It won't?"

But this time Ardella knew exactly what Marney meant. Decisions could be changed—one could quit a job, divorce a husband, sell a house or cancel a vacation. Changing these decisions might have a cost, but they could be changed. Decisions had to be made but they didn't always have to be stuck to.

And any decision was often better than no decision at all. At least that way you felt at least partly in control of your life.

The same thing was true with mistakes.

Marney dumping a bucket of fish on the Old Man's shoes was a mistake she'd obviously overcome. Ardella took heart from that thought—if she made a mistake, she'd get over it or past it or around it. Somehow.

"You're right," Ardella finally admitted to Marney. And to

herself. "When I was twenty I believed everything—from what shirt to wear or whether to get my hair cut—was of the absolute importance, so much so that at times I was paralyzed, couldn't make any decision at all."

"I remember once," Marney laughed, "when I cancelled a date with a boy I wanted so badly I dreamed of him every night for a year."

"Why?"

"Because I couldn't decide whether to wear a bra or not. Would it be too obvious if I didn't? Too awkward if I did? Stupid. But that kind of thing happened to me all the time back then."

"Me, too. But it won't happen to me now." Ardella crossed her fingers behind her back for luck and pushed open the door into her brand-new kingdom.

The smell already seemed familiar to her, as if she'd spent years of her life living with it in her nostrils, as if her brain welcomed it. The aromas rested at the back of her tongue, a little less obvious than their scent in her nose, but she tasted them.

The rich saltiness of the ocean, distilled down in the tanks to its essence. Wet concrete, reminiscent of summer rain on asphalt after a long dry spell. Brine and fish. You couldn't smell the live ones, but the scent of the feed overlay everything in the working tunnels of the aquarium. From the tiniest of shrimp to pieces of thirty-pound salmon, the smell of fish was everywhere.

And then there was the smell of the lush tropical greenery, faint under the stronger aromas. It blew in whenever the door into the Amazon rain forest opened or shut.

Ardella inhaled it as if it were life to her and she thought it might be, this particular combination of scents and flavors.

Then there was the light, filtered through glass, reflected off water, rippling through the air, turning it into something she could almost touch.

Ardella's heart pounded in her chest, an unmanageable grin on her face. She was here and today she was going to work.

And she did.

She learned how to filet fish, to weigh shrimp, to read the feeding schedules and lists. She learned how to shift fifty-pound buckets from trucks to freezers. She learned how to use her shoulder to scratch her nose after half a dozen times of smearing fish guts on her face and sneezing scales for an hour afterward.

She learned that her body contained muscles she'd never used before and she learned that blisters could and did reform in places where they'd only just burst.

She learned that while white shorts and running shoes were standard garb, they didn't last long at this job and she resolved to buy a dozen pairs of shorts—the five pairs she bought before she started work would never see her through the summer.

She learned that Terry and Joe and Nick were funny and cheerful enough that she could—at least temporarily—ignore the blisters and aching muscles and she learned that even hidden in the dungeons—Joe's term—Ardella could think of nowhere else she'd rather be.

The day, and the ones following it, passed so quickly she could barely keep track. She knew when Fridays came because the four of them—usually accompanied by Marney and occasionally by Greg Angus—treated themselves to fish and chips and a beer or two at Lumberman's Arch.

GREG ANGUS WORKED very hard at that *occasionally*. He didn't want to scare Ardella, didn't want her to know how quickly he'd fallen for her. He'd seen her standing with the other volunteers and the look on her face reeled him in, hook, line and sinker.

He'd gone home that night and couldn't remember what color her hair was, or her eyes, but the look on her face? It killed him. She looked excited and scared and nervous all at once. And on top of all those emotions rolling over her face in waves, one emotion stood out. Greg recognized it because he'd felt it himself the day he started work at the aquarium. Love.

And for the first time in months, for the first time since they'd forced him away from the ocean, he felt grateful to be on dry land.

Ardella had to know he was interested, how could she not? No matter what he was doing, no matter what she was doing, he made sure to run into her every couple of hours. He laughed at his strategy. He used all the skills he'd learned working with dolphins and sea lions in the wild. He wanted her accustomed to his presence before he moved in, before he got close enough to study her, to get to know her.

At first, she acted just as the sea creatures did, turning away when he showed up, but as she got used to his presence, she began to look forward to visits. Sometimes she even talked to him.

But Greg Angus hadn't spent twenty years with wild creatures for nothing. He knew exactly how often to show up, when he needed to back off, when she was uncomfortable with his presence, and when he needed to push—just a little.

*Fish and chips at Lumberman's Arch was a perfect example. She seemed to be fine with him showing up *occasionally* but she wasn't ready to see him every Friday night. That would be too much like a date. And she wasn't ready for that. He could tell.

ARDELLA LOVED Friday nights, especially the ones when Greg Angus wasn't around to make her uncomfortable in her own skin. It didn't matter if it was sunny—they ate on a blanket on the grass—or raining—they huddled at one of the few picnic tables under the sloped roof of the fish and chips shop. The fish and chips and the beer were their treat for making it through the week.

It was the only time she left her apartment except to go to work. She even ordered her groceries online and had them delivered. She was just too tired—and too smelly—for anything else.

And showers didn't help at all. She'd come home on Friday nights, thanking her landlord for having those monstrous hot water tanks in the basement. By Sunday night, she could almost bear herself, but the rest of the time she had to force herself into the shower.

The heat and humidity pulled the fish smell out of her pores until she felt as if she were standing in a pile of three-day-old dead fish. Breathing through her mouth helped only a little.

If she couldn't bear the smell, no one else should have to.

She wondered about Marney and Greg who, not spending their days in the dungeons slinging fish, weren't quite as aromatic as the four volunteers, but decided in the end that they'd lived with it so long they were used to it. She saw no hint of disgust on either of their faces.

Joe, though, didn't worry about the smell at all.

"My wife—" Ardella had been shocked the first time he said those two words, thinking him far too young to be married "—my wife," he'd said, a smile lighting his face, "grew up in a fishing village. The smell doesn't bother her, not a bit."

Ardella envied him having someone besides a goldfish to talk to. Even when she was very sick, her mother had been a talker. She talked about the books she'd read, the TV program she'd watched, the radio interview she'd heard in the middle of the night. Ardella missed that running commentary on life.

But the aquarium and—as much as hated to admit it— Greg Angus helped make up for the silence of her apartment.

CHAPTER 5

Belugas or Arctic white whales
(Delphinapterus leucas):
Small flippers and tail flukes
help them stay warm in
cold Arctic waters.

The long summer days rolled into each other and Ardella settled into her new home. Her muscles still ached at the end of the day but now a long shower was enough to soothe the worst of it.

A good night's sleep on her clean linens completed the rehabilitation.

Ardella couldn't remember ever enjoying the mornings so much. She'd thought of herself as a night person, watching the late late show and dragging herself out of bed around ten or ten-thirty and then taking another hour to be human.

But that was no longer true.

She jumped out of bed at six, showered, cooked bacon and eggs and hash browns—she'd had to learn how to make breakfast because she was sure she'd never done it before. She and her mother always planned lunch as the first meal of the day.

Ardella wondered how much of her behavior—behavior she'd always considered as much a part of her as the color of her eyes—was really *her's* and not her mother's.

She guessed this summer would go a long way toward finding out.

When her mother had finally—after twenty years of coping with her illness—given up the struggle, it had taken Ardella months before she'd changed a single thing.

Mourning, Ardella thought of those months. The Victorians had the right idea, forcing survivors to take the time to get over their loss before moving on with their life. Because those months of sameness had worked for Ardella.

One day, almost eight months after her mother had died, she woke up. Not in the morning but in the middle of the afternoon. Not in bed but out in the world. She woke up as if she'd spent the last months in some sort of dream state.

She was walking along the Seawall when she looked up and saw her future. It came to her in a roar, an almost unbearably intense cascade of desires and thoughts and plans.

She'd walked halfway around the park—and far past her usual turning-around point—before she'd sorted it all out.

She walked and the sky was bluer, the air more exhilarating, the water more inviting. She took off her shoes and socks to walk on the beach, to stand at the water's edge and feel the rough sand scraped away beneath her feet by the power of the ocean.

Ardella ignored the risk to her clothing and sat on a damp log while she planned her life, not noticing the cold or hearing the voices of the people walking or running or cycling the Seawall behind her.

The planning didn't take long because it was all there, as if it had been percolating for the previous eight months and was now brewed to perfection.

She knew what she would do, how and when she would do it. She could see—for the first time since she was a teenager—what she wanted her life to be and how she was going to get there.

She'd sell the condo, pay off all the bills and still have a nest egg, albeit a very small one. She'd rent an apartment downtown, close to buses for school and close to the aquarium for everything else.

She'd work at the aquarium in the summers and maybe at term breaks—she'd use her nest egg to live on, for books and tuition, to get to her dream job.

She'd get her degree in marine biology and then she'd work full-time at the aquarium for the rest of her life.

Ardella sat on a log that cool winter day and saw the rest of her life spread out before her, just as the ocean filled the world in front of her, right to the horizon. Sure it might be rough at times—storms and rain and wind—but the ocean was big enough to roll right over those things and so was she.

She was prepared to do whatever it might take to live her postponed life, work as hard as necessary, sleep as little as required, study harder than every other student.

This was her chance, her shot, and she would do whatever it took to make her dream come true.

There was just one little problem.

CHAPTER 6

Sea otters (Enhydra lutris):
Have thick fur to keep them warm
instead of fat or blubber. They
spend a lot of time floating
at the surface grooming their fur
or sleeping.

Ardella's years so far had ill-prepared her for a social life, even the limited kind of one involved in a job where she worked mostly with three kids young enough to be her sons and daughter.

Applying for a place at university was simple in comparison, though the requisite interview—needed if she applied as a mature student—was the tiniest bit hair-raising. But it was nowhere near as tough as her first few weeks at the aquarium had been.

Every morning she had to convince herself to walk up to the door. Every morning she had to fight her ingrained shyness to carry on conversations with her co-workers. Every morning she had to resist the urge to quit, to walk up out of the dungeons and into Greg Angus's office.

Every time she saw him she'd been tempted to say, "I can't do this," and every time she resisted the temptation. She'd also been tempted to say, "What are you doing after work?" but she resisted that as well.

And now, weeks into the summer, she no longer thought of quitting, no longer had to work to talk to even complete strangers, no longer struggled with shyness.

In fact, she thought with a grin, if I keep this up, I'll soon rival Marney or Greg in the talking department. Soon *they* won't be able to get a word in edgewise.

Because the real Ardella had shown up, shining through the facade, the wall of double-wide bricks and dense mortar, that had built up over those twenty lonely years. The real Ardella was a whole new person.

Or maybe a new and improved version of the person she'd almost been at twenty. A person tempered through sorrow and caring and hard, sad work.

Take this week, for example.

She'd spent her first weeks at the aquarium in the kitchen, named so, once again, by Joe, who'd shared her duty. Though the aquarium called it the fish house, the four of them ignored the others and called it the kitchen. It took Joe and Ardella six hours every day to prepare the food for all the creatures in this huge space.

Then it took them many more hours each week to offload the supplies that made their continuous way to the loading ramp. Running the aquarium was a much bigger and more complicated job than Ardella had imagined.

But today was celebration day.

This Monday she and Joe would switch jobs with Nick and Terry. They would move further up in the tunnels and begin the round of cleaning and refilling the tanks. There was an ongoing schedule, ensuring that every tank, every pool, every rock and piece of glass got cleaned regularly.

Ardella could hardly wait. Even with the extra hours she put in on the weekends watching the sea otters or seals or belugas in their outdoor pools, she missed the dazzling light that seemed visible only in the aquarium. Now she'd get to spend almost all her day as part of the light she'd fallen in love with.

GREG HAD BEEN DELIGHTED when it became time to switch the volunteer duties. Now he wouldn't have to search out Ardella in the back alleys and dungeons of the building. She'd be visible all the time. Much easier to find her in the upper part of the building, much less obvious when he showed up at her side.

He'd found her, as he often did, leaning over the sea otter pool, the sun lighting up her hair, her grin as big as the Pacific.

He couldn't blame her. No matter how unhappy or worried he was, watching the otters made him smile. They played with each other, played to the audience, played with their food, just like seagoing puppies. Or babies. Everyone loved them.

Especially Ardella.

"Hey," he said, warning her of his arrival.

"Hey, yourself," she said, without turning her head away from the pool.

Greg surprised himself. He'd come out to see her face, talk to her about her new job, but found himself talking about something he never spoke about.

"It's my mom's birthday today," he said. "I miss her, you know, all the time."

"How long?" Ardella's voice was as steady as his was not.

"Since forever. I was almost nineteen. Now there's just me and my brother, Bobby. My dad lives in England, moved there right after Mom died. We never see him."

"Where does Bobby live?"

Greg shook off the lingering sorrow and smiled at the interest in her voice. "He's a vagabond, a musician. He travels all over, looking for the next gig. No money in it, but he's happy. So between me being somewhere on the ocean and him being wherever it is he's interested in this year, we don't see much of each other. But we talk a lot, use e-mail and phone calls."

"It's nice to have family."

"You don't have any?"

"No, just my mom and she's gone now."

He watched as she wiped a tear from her eye and then turned to face him. The smile on her face…God, he wasn't sure he could stop himself. But he did.

"Tell me about your brother."

"I'll do even better," he said, once again surprised at himself. "I'll bring him with me on Friday night."

CHAPTER 7

Black ghost knifefish
(Apteronotus albifrons):
A jet-black eel-like fish,
it can swim backwards and
forwards. Some believe these
fish hold the souls of their ancestors.

Being in the light was great, though there were days...

Days when every time she turned around, she found Greg Angus. Days when he forced her to talk to him—about her life, about her dreams, even about her mother. The one thing she didn't talk about.

And then he talked to her—and she wanted to hear him. This was not going well. Or it was going too well. She wasn't sure which.

She had a pat answer for any questions about why she was going back to school at forty. "I've been busy," she'd say, "but mostly," with a grin that fooled almost everyone, "I've just figured out what I want to be when I grow up."

That made everyone who asked that question laugh and they let her go. They didn't just let her go, they grinned back at her. Ardella was used to that response, she'd come to expect it.

So when she tried the line on Greg Angus she knew exactly what he'd do. He'd grin that big gorgeous grin of his and he'd laugh that belly laugh and then walk away.

Except he didn't.

"I read your application, remember? I know why you're doing this now and I really respect that. Most people—" he paused for a minute as if remembering something he didn't like "—don't have the courage to start something this late in life. Most people—" he paused again, looking down at the Steller sea lions in the pool in front of them "—just give up."

Ardella wasn't sure what to say to that. So she reached out and touched the back of his hand. He looked up from his contemplation of the sea lions and shook his head, slightly. Ardella recognized that gesture, having often made it herself. She needed to remember that Greg Angus wasn't only the happy guy she'd seen at work, that he, too, had a past, a complicated one.

She turned his hand over and tucked it into hers, squeezing it for reassurance. And she wasn't sure whether the reassurance was for her or for Greg. *Maybe both*, she thought.

SHE'D FINALLY DONE IT, finally begun to see him as a man and not just another problem she had to solve to get to her goal. He'd been waiting weeks for that touch and now that it had happened, Greg had absolutely no idea what to do about it.

He was pretty sure Ardella didn't know what it meant, but he did. And he'd played out all kinds of scenarios for what he'd do when she finally touched him.

None of them were going to work. He was just going to have to go with his instincts. And Greg Angus had great instincts.

He tugged on her hand to pull her a little closer, not close enough to scare her, just near enough that he could feel the warmth from her body, smell the scent of her.

And then he took a big risk. He took the hand she'd given him and raised it to his lips.

"Thank you," he said. And kissed it again, savoring the taste of her.

He started counting—one, two, three. He figured he'd get to ten before she pulled away, but he was wrong again. Ardella Simpson was ignoring all of his plans. He made it as far as five, enjoying the blush on her cheeks and the warmth of her skin on his lips, before she moved back, taking her hand and her warmth with her.

And then she ran. Right across the courtyard and—he guessed—right down to the fish house.

He grinned. She didn't know it, but today's touch was just the beginning.

CHAPTER 8

Steller sea lions (Eumetopias jubatus):
Highly gregarious, they spend time
on rock shelves, ledges, boulders
and beaches for resting and breeding.
They eat about six percent of their
body weight every day.

Greg Angus had kissed her hand as if he didn't even notice the smell. And she'd bet he didn't. He'd spent all his life around sea creatures—he probably liked her aroma.

This job gave her an excuse to indulge her favorite passion— baths. She bought cinnamon scented candles and placed them around the tub and then picked bars of soap from the baskets.

She laughed and thought of her bathroom counters piled high with baskets full of soap. Sweet soap. Glycerin soap. Soap made specially for mechanics. Soap with granules of some harsh substance to get grease off. Soap with deep-cleaning properties. Goat's milk soap. Honey soap. At least one bar of every single brand of soap sold at her local drugstore.

Once she'd picked the soap—or soaps—of the day, she turned off the light, turned on the CD player—usually Bach or some kind of new age water music—and lay back in the water, dreaming of Greg Angus. Okay, okay, she had to admit it, when he told her about his mother and his brother Bobby, she'd fallen. She'd been hanging on by her fingernails up until then, but now? She was in love.

She shrugged her shoulders, rolling them backward and forward to eliminate the tension she felt just thinking those words. It didn't mean that she had to do anything about it, did it? It didn't mean she'd have to give up her first love for her second, did it?

Ardella had planned her life so carefully, so perfectly. She wrote it down, she put a copy of the list on her fridge, on her bathroom mirror, inside her locker at work. Affirmations. Proof she would make it.

Volunteer at the aquarium.

School.

Study.

Full-time employee of the aquarium.

Happy.

No relationship in that plan, especially not a relationship with the *co-director*. That would be a very bad idea.

Ardella had reheated the bath water half a dozen times before she made a decision. She would stick to her plan, to her first love. She'd be fine without Greg Angus, she'd been fine without a man this far, she could do it. Really.

SHE RAN INTO Marney on Monday morning as she hurried down to the security door—Marney running because, as usual, she was fifteen minutes behind schedule.

"Hmm, let's see," she said. "I smell apple and jasmine." She leaned in closer and took a whiff. "Is that Ivory soap?"

Ardella nodded, embarrassed.

"And Chanel No. 5 soap? Where did you get the money for that?"

"I didn't buy it. Mom gave it to me for Christmas years ago. I just hadn't used it before."

"Okay, and then there's some kind of drugstore brand for men, right? Irish Spring or something like that?"

"I admit it. Last night I took half a dozen bars of soap into the bath with me and I used all of them."

"And bubble bath? I used to try all kinds of bubble baths. From the cheapest ones in the drugstore to the expensive ones from Holt Renfrew. None of them ever worked."

"No bubble bath, not last night. I took the soaps, cut them up into tiny slices—I'm getting really good at that—and then put them under the spray. Lots and lots and lots of bubbles.

"And then I bundled up all the leftovers into a single bar and used that this morning."

Marney laughed. "You're much more ingenious than me, though—" she leaned in to smell her again "—you don't smell much better."

Ardella loved the smell of her bathroom in that moment before she turned on the shower, when all the aromas were still distinct, and then she loved it even more when they all mushed together into something new and precisely *Ardella*.

And despite the perfume and her determination to go with her first love instead of Greg, he still followed her around. She often found him waiting for her at the summer students' table at lunchtime or trolling the dungeons for her in the middle of the afternoon.

She wasn't sure what to make of him, of his obvious interest in her, except to suppose it was that she was practically the only person in the entire place who was close to his age. There were a few administrative people who had probably been there for a while, a few of the senior staff who were his age, but she was the one he followed.

She couldn't be falling in love with him. That would ruin everything.

Ardella had her life mapped out and she wasn't interested in taking any more detours. The route was all laid out, day by day, year by year, and nothing was going to interfere this time.

Not even Greg Angus.

GREG COULDN'T HELP HIMSELF. Every morning he got out of bed and spoke to his rumpled self in the bathroom mirror.

"You have to stop following her," he said. "It doesn't matter that she used to talk to you. She doesn't anymore."

He scraped the hair from his chin, puffed out his cheeks and spoke around the puffs. "And she has a plan." The crease between his eyebrows—the one that meant *huh?*—deepened. "How do I know that? Because she talks about it every single day.

"Because she spends every single spare minute and at least one day every weekend following the aquarists around. We've never had a volunteer who's more committed to her job than Ardella. *That's* how I know she has a plan."

She hadn't talked to him about it. She hardly spoke to him at all anymore. She smiled at him but she *spoke* to the other volunteers, just not when he was in the group. Occasionally, and he cringed at the thought of his foolishness, he sat at the table behind the volunteers, his back to Ardella and he listened to their conversations.

He knew, and not just from the résumé he'd pulled from her file, that she was going to university in the fall. He knew that she'd wanted to be a marine biologist since she was a teenager, for most of her life.

He understood that desire. He'd never wanted anything else. Or anything more. Until he met Ardella Simpson.

He knew as much about her as it was possible to know until he somehow convinced her to talk to him. He knew she lived in a tiny, relatively cheap—in Vancouver there were no cheap rents—apartment so she could spend the summer working at the aquarium for nothing, knew she hoarded every penny in her savings account so it would get her through four years of school.

But they had a connection. He knew it. He knew too much about her not to realize that she'd backed off once she saw that connection.

He knew she liked burgers, loved fries with salt and vinegar, drank beer from the bottle. She smelled like all the perfumes of Araby—Greg laughed at that image because he was sure that when he'd started volunteering at the aquarium he'd probably smelled exactly the same way—on Monday mornings.

The rest of the time she smelled like home to him. She smelled like the ocean.

CHAPTER 9

Brooding anenome (Epiactis prolifera):
These long-lived flowerlike creatures are
predators. They have no skeletons, live attached
to sea floor, rock or coral but can
slide around very slowly.

The next few weeks passed so quickly Ardella was astonished when she looked up from her book one Saturday night to find it would soon be August and her stint at the aquarium was winding its way down to the end.

After the incident—she couldn't think of anything else to call it—at the sea lion pool, Ardella had backed off even further from Greg. She gave up the Friday-night fish and chips because he was always there. She stopped eating lunch in the courtyard and took her lunch out of the aquarium and onto the grass opposite the pools.

It slowed him down a little, she thought, though it didn't exactly stop him. He had an uncanny ability to find her, no matter what tank or pool she was cleaning.

She'd be hidden in the back of the Treasures of the BC Coast and he'd walk by. Or she'd be hiding out in the kitchen and he'd find her there. She wondered if he'd put a secret transmitter in her sneakers or something, but seeing as she had to change them every few weeks, that probably wasn't it.

Even when she went down into Clownfish Cove, braving the screams and giggles of the dozens of kids who loved the place, he wandered in. He smiled at all the children, bending down to answer their questions, often getting caught up in some game they were playing.

He was like a big kid himself.

And she felt that big kid right behind her. He'd followed her out of the aquarium and into the shade of the huge cedar she'd chosen as her lunchtime retreat.

She wasn't safe from him even out of the aquarium.

But when he sprawled on the grass beside her and grinned, she smiled back at him and passed him the cardboard container of fries.

"I know, I know, there's probably too much salt and vinegar on them."

"Nope, never too much for me," he said, and proceeded to eat the whole top layer of fries, the ones with the most salt, most vinegar, the best ones.

"You could at least pretend you didn't want them," Ardella said. "I bought them for myself."

"I'll buy you some more, I promise. But it's been a rough week and I need the sustenance."

The dark circles around his eyes matched the black T-shirt he wore. Ardella hadn't seen much of him—at least in the daylight—in the past week what with hiding out in the dungeons. And when he did find her, it was pretty dark back there and she ran as soon as she could.

"Everything okay?" she said against her better judgment. She shouldn't be talking to him, he was just too tempting.

"Hmm," he said, "delicious," licking the salt and vinegar from his fingers.

Her eyes followed the fingers and then darted away. "I mean other than the fries." She wanted to add the words *you idiot* but restrained herself, not because he was the co-director, but because it was too personal.

She'd spent her grown-up life with an ill mother and not many other people. Teasing was something she was still working on and she'd still only managed it with a few people. Marney, Joe, Terry, Nick. They were it.

So she quelled the impulse to do it with Greg and waited to see if he'd answer her. If not, she'd pick up her blanket and head back to work.

"Busy," he said, sprawling back on the grass, his arms over his face.

"Nope, it's not just that. You *like* to be busy."

"Could I ask you not to ask?"

"You could, but I won't listen. You could tell me that you don't want to talk about it."

A smile appeared from beneath his crossed arms. "I could, but the trouble is I do want to talk. To you. And if this is my only choice…"

She interrupted him. "It is." Ardella thought about running and then thought, *what the hell.* "Come on, Greg, tell me what's up. You look terrible."

He sat up and rubbed his fingers through his hair. Now instead of a serious co-director, he looked like a little boy who'd been caught in a hedge while playing tag.

She reached out to smooth down the wayward hair, but stopped herself just in time. She remembered how it felt the last time she touched Greg Angus. Better not to try it again.

"Is it work?"

Ardella didn't have all day. Even if she was out here playing *tell me if you can* with the co-director, she still had a whole pile of things on her schedule before the end of the day.

"Not work."

"Okay, that's enough. I don't have time to drag this out of you. You want to talk to me, try saying more than two words at a time. I have to get back to work in—" she looked at her watch "—half an hour. Get your mouth in gear and tell me the damned problem."

HE SAT UP, crossed his legs, settled his forearms on his thighs and squared his shoulders. This wasn't going to be easy. Social he might appear, but he was a pretty reserved kind of guy about stuff that really mattered.

"You know about my brother Bobby. He's ten years younger than me and I practically brought him up after Mom died. Menopause baby, I guess. Mom called him her miracle baby."

Ardella nodded encouragement when he slowed down. "And?"

"He's sick. And they can't figure out what it is. Some kind of virus, they say. But he just keeps getting weaker and weaker.

He's on super-strength drugs, getting fed through a tube, and he's still losing weight. I swear, Ardella, he's lost twenty pounds this week alone."

She reached out her hand and rested it on his arm. "What are they doing next?"

"They've sent samples to be tested. They think it's some kind of African virus, but they have no idea how to treat it. And there's nothing I can do."

There was the crux of it, he thought. He couldn't help his baby brother and he'd always looked out for him. Always. That had been his job since the day Bobby was born.

He tucked Ardella's hand into his and felt comforted by the warmth of it. He felt the calluses she'd acquired over the past couple of months, the deep indentations growing on her soft skin from immersion in salt water, from cutting up herring and squid and mackerel.

In lots of ways, he missed the last time he'd worked on dry land, when he'd worked on the floor of the aquarium instead of in the executive offices. He missed the daily contact with the kids, missed the feel of the water on his hands, missed… Well, he missed a lot of it.

But most of all, right now, he was sick to death with worry about Bobby.

"That's why I haven't seen much of you this week," Ardella said, her voice low and sweet. "You've been at the hospital."

"Yes."

"Why don't you go now? Meet me at the bar in the Sylvia at seven o'clock, I'll buy you a drink and you can tell me how he is today."

ARDELLA COULDN'T BELIEVE she'd offered to buy him a drink but it was too late to take it back. And the look on Greg's face was worth whatever qualms she'd suffer until seven o'clock.

He looked as if she'd given him a gift. And she guessed that maybe she had.

CHAPTER 10

Reid's seahorse (Hippocampus reidi):
These small fish have armored plates
(not scales). The female seahorse
produces eggs but they are held
inside the male's body until they hatch.
This is the only animal in which the
father is pregnant.

Ardella ran into Marney on her way back down to the dungeon, literally ran into her.

"Oh, God, sorry. I'm just not paying attention."

"Obviously not." Marney laughed. "And why is that?"

Marney had spent a fair amount of time over the past couple of months teasing her about what she called "Greg's obvious crush." And Marney knew everything Ardella did, in or out of work. She just *knew*.

Two weeks into her new job, Ardella had begun to wonder whether Marney had ESP or some sort of highly trained spy network. Because she knew *everything*.

She knew Ardella never went out, except occasionally to buy new kinds of soap. She knew Joe and Kathleen spent every weekend at Kathleen's parents' house in the valley. That was one thing, but she also knew that Joe and Kathleen were trying to get pregnant. Ardella hadn't known that, and she spent hours a day with Joe.

She knew that Nick and Terry were dating, but that it wasn't serious, both of them too wrapped up in their careers to get involved at this stage of their life.

"Who do you think is going to be happier?" Marney asked her.

"Who are you talking about?"

"You know. Nick and Terry totally focused on their careers and ignoring the fact that they really care about each other. Or Joe and Kathleen. Yeah, they're keen on their careers but they're making a family."

Ardella didn't really want to answer that question because she didn't know the answer. She'd started the summer with one thing in mind—working for the rest of her life at the aquarium. Sure, she had to go university to do that, but it was all about the aquarium for her.

The summer hadn't changed her mind about that, but she had realized a few weeks ago that work wasn't the only thing she was thinking about.

Damn that Greg Angus, getting into her head like that.

"Ardella? What's going on in that complicated brain of yours? You thinking about Greg?"

Ardella shook her head and ignored those questions, forced by her own distraction to answer the first one.

"I don't know about Nick and Terry, but you only have to look at Joe and Kathleen to see how happy they are. I mean, they don't have any money, they're both going to school and working two jobs, they must be exhausted all the time, yet they light up when they see each other."

"They do, don't they? I'm just worried that Nick and Terry are too focused on the future to be enjoying the present. I loved being twenty—and I don't want them to miss all that fun."

Ardella waited for the punch line. Marney wasn't just talking about the kids, she was talking about Ardella. She didn't wait long.

"You, too."

"Me, too, what?" Ardella didn't really think that it would stop Marney but it couldn't hurt to try. Even though nothing ever stopped Marney once she was on a roll.

She hurried down the back corridor. Maybe going right back into the tank would stop her? No; not even a good try.

Marney stood just barely inside the tank—making sure she didn't touch anything and not because she didn't want to mess up the tank but because she didn't want to mess up her white shorts and brand-new sneakers. Ardella threw her best get-over-yourself look at her.

Marney replied with, "Hey, don't get snarky about my fastidiousness. That's the reason I have a new car. I just put all that money away that I'd spend on shorts and sneakers if I weren't careful and voila. Brand-new bright red Toyota Prius."

Ardella grinned and threw a damp sponge her way, making sure to miss her by a couple of feet. "Yeah, yeah, yeah. Quit gloating, okay?"

"It's almost the end of the summer," Marney said out of nowhere. "Pretty soon your clothes will stay clean and you'll smell nice all week instead of just on Sunday nights."

"I'm trying not to think about that." Ardella's mouth opened and the words popped out before she could stop them.

Marney didn't need any help coming to conclusions. She was the queen of jumping to them and she'd long ago jumped to the Greg and Ardella conclusion.

"It's not about anything except that I'm going to miss this place."

Ardella looked around at the empty tank, at the piles of stones and other accoutrements just outside the entrance. She stared out the front wall of the tank at the pale light of the Tropic Zone, knowing she'd miss this moment for months.

"I'm meeting him for a drink tonight," she finally said. "I don't know if it's a good idea or not."

"He asked you?" Marney's disbelief was almost insulting.

Ardella sniffed. "I asked him."

"Oh," Marney said. "Oh, I see."

Ardella sniffed again. "You do? Because I don't. It was a stupid idea, even if I did it for a good cause."

"Look," Marney said, stepping firmly into the tank, "it's obvious the two of you are crazy about each other. He follows you around, you watch for him every minute of the day. What can it hurt if you go on a few dates?"

"But my plan—"

"Plans can be changed."

Ardella had been forced to change her plans once and she didn't know if she could do it again. A little shift one way or the other might be okay, but Greg Angus would be a quantum leap, not some little, easily assimilated shift in her lifetime plan.

She had enough to worry about.

She still didn't know whether she'd be able to come back for a few hours a week while she was going to school. It wasn't going to be easy but she'd put in her request and was waiting— waiting for Greg to make a decision about it.

He'd already told Joe and Terry that they could work as many hours as they wanted during the school year, except Terry didn't want to and Joe wasn't sure what he was going to do, but Greg hadn't said anything to her.

Working as a volunteer at the aquarium was the thing that was going to keep her sane during the school year. She wasn't any too keen on being in a classroom with a whole bunch of eighteen-year-olds.

"You're going to miss us," Marney sang from the side of the tank where she'd retreated as soon as she'd made her point, her voice echoing around the glass. "You're going to miss me."

"I am going to miss you."

"Has Greg told you whether you can work weekends in September?"

"Nope. But he's told Joe and Terry that they can so I bet he's going to say no to me."

"But they don't want to work during the school year. I think he's just worried that it's going to be too much. You have to make at least a little money, don't you?"

"I redid my budget this weekend. If I cut back on everything—" she grinned over at Marney's gleaming white sneakers "—including clothes and eating out—not that I do much of that—I can make it through the four years."

"You can?"

"Yep. Just."

Ardella thought about the twenty hours she'd spent over the weekend balancing her new budget so she could work at the aquarium for the whole four years and not have to work anywhere else. The four years were possible without having a part-time job—just—but she'd have to get one the minute she finished school. And she wasn't kidding about that minute. She suspected she wouldn't even be able to pay her rent that final month if she didn't get a job.

But this was what she wanted, what she'd wished for her whole life. It would be worth it.

"You'd better tell Greg that. I think he's worried about you going to school, working here and having to get another part-time job. He'll probably tell you no for your own good. You know, so you'd get at least a little sleep over the winter."

"I'll tell him later on."

Ardella went back to cleaning the glass and the concrete floor, feeling the muscles she'd developed over the past couple of months. She felt good, both physically and emotionally, in a way she hadn't in so long she'd forgotten what feeling good felt like.

She was exactly where she wanted to be. She was happy right here in this smallish tank, a few kids watching her out of the corner of their eyes, Marney harassing her from the back. She was happy every night, even when she could barely stand the smell of herself as the heat of the shower intensified the aroma of her workday.

She was happy every morning, even when she woke up—

despite the Advil—with sore muscles in places she didn't know she had them.

The only problem she could see was Greg Angus. And she had no idea how she was going to solve it.

CHAPTER 11

Picasso triggerfish (Rhinecanthus aculeatus):
Eats just about anything that comes along,
swims constantly and protects territory
against intruders, including divers.

Ardella loved the bar at the Sylvia Hotel. That's why she picked it. She'd feel safe, it'd be her territory and it wasn't at all romantic.

Okay, maybe it was slightly romantic, especially in the summer. The huge windows looked out over English Bay, at the freighters, sailboats, sea kayakers and windsurfers, to where the sun was just starting to lower itself down to the mountains across the water.

The bladers and the bikers and the just-plain-wanderers filled the sidewalk and bike path across the street with color and energy.

Everyone was out on the beach. Teenage girls in giggling pods, seniors in smaller groups but just as loud, serious runners, their shorts and T-shirts matted damply to their bodies.

Seven o'clock. Seven-thirty.

Ardella finally ordered herself a glass of wine at eight o'clock and tried to concentrate on the excitement on the beach.

Family picnics, romantic dinners on a blanket for two. A handful of drummers and their fans. A man carving tiny stone bears and a woman selling a row of paintings.

Couples strolling, hand in hand, their attention on each other and not the scenery.

No Greg Angus.

Nine o'clock and another glass of wine.

"I'll wait for a few more minutes," she said to her reflection in the window. "Maybe his brother is worse and he can't leave the hospital."

Ardella still waited but now the sun was below the horizon, leaving just the faintest glow of light reflecting off the water. She waited, but mostly she worried.

Her wineglass sat empty and her stomach growled. She didn't move.

She knew herself to be a fool. It didn't matter, that foolishness, because if Greg Angus needed her, if something had happened to his brother, she wanted to be here for him.

"ARDELLA?"

Greg couldn't believe she was still waiting for him. He looked at his watch. He was three hours late and she still sat, alone, at a table by the window, an empty wineglass in front of her.

He stopped on his way over to the table and ordered a bottle of champagne. He had a lot to celebrate, not the least of which was Ardella's patience.

"Hey," he said, sliding into the chair opposite her. "You're still here."

"I was worried that something—" He saw the concern on

her face change to surprise. The grin he'd been wearing for the past several hours must still be glowing at full wattage.

"He's okay, isn't he? Bobby's going to be fine."

"He is. They got the test results back, found out what it was, and he's going to be coming home in a week or so. They want to feed him up, make sure he doesn't have an adverse reaction to the new drugs, but…"

He leaned over the table and kissed her cheek. "Thanks for waiting for me," he said. "I need to wind down a bit."

"Looks like you need to wind down a whole bunch," Ardella replied, smiling. "But my boss is an ogre—" another smile "—and I have to be at work pretty early tomorrow morning, so we can't stay too long."

"All right, but at least help me drink this bottle of champagne. I'm celebrating tonight."

ARDELLA STOPPED after the champagne and moved on to food. It was late and she was tired, but she couldn't pull herself away from the attraction she felt toward Greg. Especially now, when he was so impossibly happy.

She never thought she'd think this, let alone say it out loud, but she did.

"I wish I had someone to worry about," she said. "I miss having my mom around. I miss making sure she got to her appointments. I miss making sure she took her pills. I miss having someone…"

She had to stop or she'd cry, and that was the last thing she was going to do in front of Greg, the very last. Life was complicated enough without adding *that* complication. Men always felt uncomfortable around crying women.

At least, Ardella thought to herself, that's what the movies and books all said. So she sniffed, ignored the one tear that managed to escape, and took another sip of the glass of water in front of her.

"I think I need to get a cat. Or a dog."

She contemplated. "Okay, not a dog. I won't be home enough. But a cat would be good."

"You have fish, don't you?"

"How'd you know?"

"You told us one Friday night a few weeks ago. Nick was talking about his tank and you..."

"Oh. Well, yes, I have fish, not many, just a small tank, but I love them. Do you think the cat would eat them?"

"I don't know. But cats love movement. I mean, these are animals that chase string—fish would be irresistible. Maybe you could put the tank in your bedroom and keep the door closed?"

"I can't do that. If I get a cat, I want it to sleep on my bed. Okay, so no cat."

"But I do miss having someone to care about. Still," she brightened, "starting in a few weeks, I'll be so busy I won't have time to worry about it. Especially if—" Ardella paused and then blurted it out "—you let me work part-time during term."

Greg didn't look so happy about that, his brows almost meeting between his eyes and the lines around his mouth deepening.

"I don't think you're going to have time to do that," he said.

"I don't have anything else to do." Ardella hated admitting that to Greg. "And besides, I know the first-year material—" she didn't mention the second and third and fourth-year material "—by heart. It's going to be a snap and I don't want to leave "

She didn't want to leave the aquarium. It was home to her, not her tiny apartment.

She looked across the table at Greg Angus, at the way he cradled the glass of scotch in his hands as he looked out into the darkness. She loved his face, wanted more than ever for her face to look like his. She knew it would take years—years of working on the ocean, years of squinting into the sun, years of knowing who she was and what she was meant to do.

But she knew, too, that she'd make it. And she hoped that some day, some volunteer would walk into the aquarium and see her, and say exactly that same thing. "I want to look like her."

But even more than his face, she'd learned to love him.

She'd discovered over the summer that he was the hardest worker in the aquarium, almost never leaving before the building closed to visitors. He was there when Ardella arrived in the morning, often still there when she went home.

If she came in on the weekend—and she almost always did—Greg was there. Seldom in his temporary office, he took the opportunity to fill in for anyone who needed help or time off or who he thought looked tired. He helped with the training, he manned the volunteer carts, he worked in marine mammal rescue, he worked with the aquarists, he worked as a spotter at the beluga shows.

He loved the place as much as she did, Ardella thought. And that love was compelling as well as scary. Because he, like her, was completely focused on his work.

And if she ever had a relationship, she wanted to be first.

CHAPTER 12

Chilean rose tarantula (Grammastola rosen):
A nocturnal hunter who
finds a shelter to web itself into
at dawn.

Two weeks to go and Ardella, promoted out of the tank cleaning brigade, was now working with a volunteer cart.

She'd wanted the dolphin cart—outside in the sun, with the skull and the teeth found in the aboriginal dump—she'd ended up in the dark with the tarantula and the cockroaches.

She suspected Greg of putting her in this place. He had control of the volunteer scheduling—at least as much control as he wanted—and she thought the cockroaches might be in reprisal for her insistence on working during term.

But she'd gotten her way—and she'd barely seen him since the night at the Sylvia. They'd closed the bar, he'd walked her home, and then he'd disappeared.

He was still at work, but he didn't show up for lunch or the ongoing Friday nights at the fish and chips stand. He didn't follow her around the aquarium, didn't show up in the fish house or the dungeons.

When she did see him, he was always off in the distance somewhere, avoiding her. He was *so* obvious.

GREG WATCHED Ardella from the back of the Tropic Zone, keeping his distance. He wouldn't be surprised if she threw one of the cockroaches at him, except she was too professional to do that.

He couldn't remember another volunteer who was so committed, so professional, so knowledgeable. When she insisted that she wanted to work during the school term, there was no way for him to tell her no.

Because he couldn't tell her the real reason he didn't want her to work while she was at university. He didn't want to tell her that he worried she'd be too busy for him.

He'd resolved to wait until September before he asked her out. And there were only two weeks to go.

He wasn't sure he could wait that long.

He smiled as he watched Ardella with the kids clamoring around the cart. She laughed and chatted with them as if they were her best friends, and maybe they were.

She was much more comfortable with them than she was with him. All summer she'd been avoiding him, except for that one day when he told her about Bobby.

And that one night they'd spent in the bar at the Sylvia Hotel, Ardella sitting across the table from her, her eyes shining in the candlelight, laughing with him, drinking champagne to celebrate.

That was a perfect night.

But before and after that night? Nothing. A big fat zero. He knew she was aware of him, could feel her breath catch, her body tense, when he came up next to her. But she fought it, fought it big-time.

It was almost September. If he could wait that long.

ARDELLA KNEW he was watching her, she always knew when he was watching her. Greg was somewhere at the back of the room, just out of comfortable reach of her eyesight in the dim light of the big fish room.

She could see the caiman, sleeping as always. She didn't think she'd seen that creature move more than two or three times in the past couple of months. He loved the water, but he didn't swim in it, or if he did, it was at night when the building was closed to visitors.

Maybe he was shy, she thought, maybe he just didn't like people. Or maybe, she laughed inside at the thought, he liked people too much. Maybe he saw them as food. All those kids had to be mighty tempting, their giggles and their warm little bodies.

She wouldn't want to be a caiman in this world. No way. Except that he got fed regularly and he got to be as lazy as he wanted to be. Maybe that made up for the excitement of the real world.

"What's up?"

Ardella jumped and almost dropped the tarantula—and that would be the equivalent of dropping a bucket of fish on the director's shoes. Marney had snuck up on her while she was watching out for Greg.

"I just about lost the bloody tarantula. Don't scare me like that."

"Sorry, I didn't realize you were so engrossed. And what were you engrossed in?"

Marney turned until she saw—and Ardella saw that she saw—the door heading out of the Tropic Zone closing behind Greg Angus.

"It all makes sense now. And get that bug out of my sight. You know I hate bugs."

"You don't like Rose?"

Ardella held the tarantula, its legs long and covered with silky hair, out to Marney, who shuddered and backed away.

"No. I don't."

"What about the cockroaches?"

Ardella put Rose back in her case and reached for the cockroaches. It had taken her a few days to get used to holding the big shiny black bugs in her hand, but now they just tickled and didn't scare her.

"I'm outta here. Right now."

Ardella watched Marney practically run for the exit and then listened for a minute, tuning out the soft laughter of the kids drooling over the tarantula she'd picked up again.

She heard the soft sounds of the scarlet ibis in the room next door, the drip-drip of the pipes on the roof of the rain forest room.

She didn't hear Greg's booming laugh—which was unusual because wherever he was, she usually heard him laughing. He laughed all the time. And she was trying to follow his example.

This summer had been a real revelation. She'd expected hard work. She'd expected excitement. She'd expected the fear of trying something knew. She'd expected anxiety.

And she'd felt all of those things.

What she hadn't expected was the joy. And the friendship.

She hadn't expected the happiness and comfort she felt in this place, with these people.

And more than anything else, she hadn't expected the temptation of Greg Angus. Well, she was just going to keep resisting it.

She had her plan and she was sticking to it. It had taken her twenty-seven years to get here—from her thirteenth summer to her fortieth—and there was no way she was going to give up everything she'd ever dreamed of for a *man*.

Even a man as attractive and funny and perfect as Greg Angus. Not even for him.

CHAPTER 13

Spectacled caiman (Caiman crocodiles):
Caiman is a Spanish term for alligator. They are
large, meat-eating reptiles that spend most
of their lives in the water, including the Amazon basin.

"One week to go," Marney said as she pressed the buzzer for the security guard to open the back door. "And then you'll be at school every day. Looking forward to it?"

She didn't let Ardella answer that question.

"Of course you are. But I bet you're going to miss being here every day. You're going to miss me, right?"

"Yes, I'll miss you, but we've already decided that you'll meet me every Tuesday for dinner. So I won't miss you *that* much."

Ardella laughed at the expression on Marney's face. She'd expected her to say… What? She'd expected her to talk about Greg, she guessed. Well, that topic was out of bounds.

"You're going to miss the kids, too. Joe and Nick and Terry. And Kathleen."

Ardella and Marney had gotten to know Kathleen over the summer. She met them—really, she met Joe—for fish and chips every Friday night. Mostly because the two of them couldn't wait to see each other.

When she and Joe walked home together during the week, Ardella could see from a block away Kathleen sitting, her head swivelled to watch the street, on the stoop of their apartment building. She could have waited for Joe in the apartment, but that would mean another few minutes without him.

And when she saw him? When they saw each other?

Joe didn't even bother to say goodbye, he just took off running down the street, Kathleen doing the same from the stoop, and they'd meet in the middle, arms reaching for each other as if they hadn't seen each other for days, instead of only ten hours.

Ardella watched this same scene enacted four days a week for the whole summer and she still loved it. Loved the way Kathleen screamed when she finally spotted Joe, loved the way Joe ran, even at the end of an excruciatingly hard day, as if he couldn't wait another minute to have Kathleen in his arms.

"I'm going to miss the kids, but I'll see Joe and Kathleen over the winter. Joe and I might hit a few shifts together and we've already decided to have drinks or dinner together when we can fit it in."

"It's going to be hard, you not being here every day," Marney said. "I swear I spend more time here than I do at home and I loved you being here."

Ardella smiled and waited for the next Marney onslaught, hoping she wouldn't mention Greg, because she had absolutely no idea how to respond to any questions about him.

"The new food services people are doing a pretty good job, but it's all too healthy. I'm going to miss the fish and chips.

Once they close down the Lumberman's Arch stand, there isn't a place around for *real* food."

Marney's idea of real food was plenty of grease and salt. Ardella suspected their weekly dinners would consist of burgers, beer, fish and chips, maybe the occasional stop at KFC. Both of them were addicted to grease and salt, though Marney wasn't a real vinegar fan.

"We can find a place that serves fish and chips downtown somewhere."

"It won't be the same. You need to eat them outside for the perfect effect."

Marney smiled, ruffled Ardella's hair and said, "I'll see you at lunchtime. Have fun with the cockroaches."

Marney had come by that once to see the cockroach show and then conspicuously stayed away the rest of the time. Bugs were not on Marney's list of fun things to see or do.

Marney's favorite things? The belugas in the big pool at the aquarium. She loved them and Ardella was willing to swear they loved her back.

When she passed the pool, all of them followed her, their heads out of the water, their eyes following her every move. When she leaned down over the blue water, they were there, waiting for her.

If she was down in the underground viewing area giving her spiel about the belugas, it was hard for the trainers to convince them to do their routine. They wanted to be where they could see Marney. Splashing the customers wasn't anywhere near as entertaining as following Marney around the pool.

Ardella wondered why Marney hadn't become an aquarist

or a trainer. The belugas loved her—they'd do anything she asked of them. And so did the sea lions and the sea otters. Even the sharks seemed to accept her company when she—very occasionally—worked with them.

But then she thought about the way people's eyes lit up when Marney told them about Lancaster Sound or the Amazon rivers or how seahorses had babies. She thought about Marney's face when she spoke to the tiniest of children and she knew exactly why Marney did what she did.

She didn't want to do anything else.

Ardella only hoped that her face—like Marney's and like Greg's—would begin to reflect the joy and passion they felt in their lives. She thought she was well on her way to getting there.

She could see it in the mirror—the difference between her old face and her new one. It wasn't that her skin was clearer or her eyes were brighter or her smile bigger, though it was all of that.

Ardella stood in front of the mirror in the changing room, the fluorescent lights glaring, and she examined the face in the mirror. It was still *her* face but it was at the same time a new face.

She'd acquired some fine lines around her eyes, because mostly every day she forgot her sunglasses and spent half the day squinting against the sun.

She'd changed color to reflect her surroundings, just like the chameleons in the rain forest room. Her skin was darker, slightly tanned. Warm.

And her eyes? Yes, they were brighter, but they were also more focused, more intense. Because Ardella now knew she'd made the right decision that day on the beach. The scrimping and saving over the next four years weren't going to matter nor were the eighty-hour weeks. The Ardella she saw in the mirror was a woman on a mission, a woman with a goal.

And it was a goal she was passionate about. No more endurance, no more just making it. Every single day would be an adventure, every single day a joy.

And all of that—not to mention the fact that maybe, just maybe, for the first time in her life she might be falling in love—was reflected in her face.

Ardella thought back over the summer. She'd made friends, she worked in the place she'd always dreamed of being, and she'd met Greg Angus. She definitely hadn't expected that. Meeting the co-director was one thing. Knowing he wanted to spend time with her was another. Knowing she might be falling in love with him? That was frightening and wonderful and painful all at once.

CHAPTER 14

Humbug dascyllus (Dascyllus aruanus):
Loves reefs, eats plankton, benthic
invertebrates and algae. Very aggressive.

Her last day before the end of summer and school and it was party time at the aquarium. The underground beluga viewing room was filled with people, everyone Ardella had met over the past summer, people she hadn't yet met because they were on a different schedule from her, people she'd only ever heard of—like the legendary founder of the aquarium.

And he even spoke to her; well, okay, he spoke to everyone. But Ardella was in her glory, here in the world she'd always wanted.

The food was amazing—seafood harvested from the cool waters of the Pacific—her ocean—and cooked by chefs from all over the world. Spring salmon cooked by Thai chefs, halibut cooked by Italian chefs and oysters prepared by African chefs.

There were photographs of the aquarium from its very inception, black-and-white ones, colored ones, photographs of the transformation of the place over the past fifty years. There was a huge poster of the stamp that celebrated the anniversary—with a portrait of one of the belugas.

A string quartet played light and airy—though she thought it should be watery—music in the background and waitstaff hired for the occasion wandered through the crowd with trays of champagne and nibbles.

Ardella had never been to a party like this in her life.

Marney stood next to her, a glass of champagne in her hand while they pretended to listen to the speeches—the founder, the mayor, the premier of the province, a senator who once was the mayor and the city's coroner, the head of the Maritime Museum, a man who still spent much of his time searching for buried treasure—celebrating the aquarium's fiftieth anniversary.

"Did you ever think you'd be here?" she asked Ardella quietly. "I mean, you've been dreaming about this for almost thirty years—God, almost as long as this place has been around—and here you are. A part of it."

Ardella smiled and whispered back, "I knew I'd be here. Knowing kept me sane all those years, kept me putting one foot in front of the other. It kept me studying so I'd be ready."

She paused for a minute, thinking back on those years. "And," she continued, "the dream of this place made me able to love my mother and not resent her. Are you kidding? Being here is like being in Oz. Or Shangri-La.

"The only thing I didn't expect is that I'd make such great friends."

She turned away so Marney couldn't see the tears in her eyes but Marney wouldn't allow it. She carefully put her glass down on the table beside them and put her arms around Ardella, the sniffles clear in her voice when she said, "I'm so glad you're here, so glad I met you."

"Hey, that's my line."

After this summer, Ardella knew that voice as well as she knew her own. Greg Angus, here at the end as he was at the beginning.

Okay, okay, it wasn't really the end, but it felt a bit that way. She'd be back in a couple of weeks, but only for one day a week. Maybe next summer she'd have the same long days of hard work—but it wasn't going to be the same without Nick and Terry and Joe.

And she wouldn't have the joy of discovering Marney, of discovering Greg, of discovering she was still a woman, a living, breathing, caring, sometimes frightened woman.

She hadn't allowed herself the luxury of those things—especially fear—for so long she almost didn't recognize it when it happened. The anxiety she'd felt on her first day, that was obvious, she'd spent twenty years experiencing it.

Ardella had felt anxious every single day, for her mother, mostly. But also about whether she'd be able to cope, whether she was capable of giving her mother the support and care she needed.

Every night she'd go to bed and worry about the next day. About the appointments, about the massages, about whether they should go for a walk and, if so, just how far her mother could manage. She worried about the menu for the next day. Would her mother be able to eat eggs? Or would a milk shake be better?

So, yes, Ardella was familiar with anxiety in all of its forms. But fear? She'd put that away for the duration. She couldn't afford it.

Now here she was, not just content, which was how she'd seen herself for all of her grown-up life, but joyful. And that was something she'd not expected.

She turned to Greg and to Marney, grabbed their hands and squeezed them.

"Thank you, both of you. I've had the best summer of my life."

She kissed Marney on the cheek, then turned to Greg. Should she or shouldn't she? Well, why the hell not?

She kissed him on the cheek.

He stopped her when she started to turn away, looking down at her with those ocean eyes, and then he smiled. And that smile contained all the secrets of the ocean, all the secrets of life, she thought.

Was she ready for them?

CHAPTER 15

Sunflower star (Pycnopodia helianthoides):
Twenty-four arms distinguish this
magnificent star from others.
Voracious predator, when on the prowl
swings along on its 15,000 tube feet,
moving faster than any other sea star at
forty inches a minute.

Greg watched Ardella as she moved through the crowd, saying goodbye to the temporary volunteers, the ones who were only with them for this one summer, saying "see you next year" to the volunteers who planned to return next summer.

He watched as she smiled at everyone, from the donors to the janitors to the women who worked in the restaurants and gift shop.

There was something different about her tonight, something he couldn't quite put his finger on. He knew what *he* was feeling—it was nostalgia, mostly.

He expected this summer to be boring but the board had said, he needed to know how they worked in the confined space of this building and not just out on the high sea.

They'd actually used the words *high seas* and Greg had laughed, planning to put in his one summer in the city and then go back out on the ship, but they'd been right. He'd learned a lot and enjoyed every minute of it.

Not all of it was attributable to Ardella, either, though she'd been a big part of reconciling him to being grounded.

Being here when Bobby was sick was another part of it. When he'd sat in the hospital for that week, waiting to see if the doctors could figure out what was wrong with his brother, he'd realized that he needed to be in one place, he needed to have a home.

If he'd been where he'd planned to be this summer—on a research vessel in Antarctica—Bobby could have died and Greg would have never seen him again. And seeing him lying on the hospital bed, so sick and frail, Greg had realized just how much he needed his brother. At least as much as Bobby needed him.

Greg and Bobby needed a home. They'd been without one for too long.

Oh, Bobby wouldn't be around much, vagabond that he was, but he needed some place to come to when he wasn't traveling. And Greg wanted that for him. And for himself. And especially, he whispered the wish, for Ardella.

Being grounded this summer had been good for him in all sorts of ways.

He'd seen the joy in children's faces as they watched the belugas and the sea otters. He'd seen what his work really meant to people and he was sure when they asked him if he wanted to stay in the city, at the aquarium instead of out on the *high seas*, he would.

He'd already been looking at houses and fighting off the desire to—before he'd officially been appointed to it—put his name on the door of the empty office next to Denise.

That didn't mean he wouldn't take the occasional trip to the Arctic or the Amazon, because he would—the waters of the world were, after all, his home. But he was pretty sure his life was going to be lived mostly right here in this city, in this building. At least, he smiled to himself, for the next four years.

ARDELLA CIRCLED THE ROOM, making sure she said goodbye to everyone she'd met over the summer. She felt beautiful and happy and without a care in the world. It was her dress, she thought, the dress Marney helped her pick out.

She wore red, brilliant fire-engine red, and it felt like a million dollars on her, though Marney—the world's best shopper—took her to a consignment store to buy it. She had insisted that Ardella dress up for the party and insisted on shopping with her.

"I don't trust you," she said. "You'll say you're going to do it and then you'll show up in a black skirt and some silk blouse you've owned for fifteen years."

Ardella laughed, because that was exactly what she'd planned to do. She didn't have spare money for clothes. But Marney had found her this dress, literally forced her to try it on, and then haggled until even Ardella couldn't resist the price.

Marney was right.

Here she was and she felt his eyes following her and she

knew exactly who it was, which man hadn't stopped watching her since she walked in the door. And it wasn't just the red dress, though maybe that was a small part of it.

Greg had seen her in shorts so filthy they were no longer white. He'd seen her cry. He'd seen her at the end of an excruciatingly long week, her hair hanging limp on her head, her eyes circled with black. He'd seen her after spending the morning fighting with a class of teenagers who were interested in anything but what she told them.

He'd seen her at her worst and he'd never once looked at her without love in his eyes.

Finally, Ardella gave in. She stopped racing around the room, stopped avoiding him.

She was careful to stop in an out-of-the-way corner and she waited while he made his way to her across the room.

Now she watched him, in his black tuxedo and brilliantly white shirt, watched while he stopped and spoke to the founder, watched the giant grin bloom on his face and was willing to bet the founder had offered him a permanent position on-site. She watched as he spoke to the volunteer coordinator and the president of the aquarium's largest corporate donor.

He was tall enough that for almost all of the conversations, he bent over to be heard through the raucous crowd, and he was beautiful enough that most of the women watched as he passed.

Ardella smiled as he burst out of the crowd and into the silent space she picked for this encounter.

"Hey," she said, holding out a glass of champagne.

"Hey," he replied, taking the glass she offered and placing it on the ledge behind him.

No more games, she thought. And she smiled up into his ocean eyes and waited.

She knew exactly what would happen. That was why she picked this isolated spot, why she'd been smiling the whole time she stood here, watching him make his way through the crowd to her.

The kiss, though, the kiss was far more than she expected.

And it was the perfect end to a perfect summer.

"It's not the end," Greg whispered, as if he read her mind. "It's the beginning."

Ardella nodded and leaned into him, knowing he was right, knowing that this summer had been the beginning of a new life for her. And it would be a much different life than the one she'd spent all those years imagining.

She'd have the work she'd always wanted, the aquarium, the creatures, the light and water and the smell of the world she craved.

She'd have friends—she smiled at the thought of Marney, of Joe and Kathleen, of Nick and Terry and all the other people she'd met over the summer, all the people she'd meet at school and over the years at the aquarium.

And she'd have a lover.

There was no doubt in his eyes as he looked at her, no question in his body as he held her, no hesitation at all as he kissed her.

She turned in Greg's arms and looked through the glass at the belugas preening for the adoring crowds. She leaned back, her head against his shoulder, and sighed.

"It's perfect," she said.

Ardella felt the rumble of his "yes" against her back and placed her hands over his. "This is my place," she said.

"It's always been your place," Greg replied, kissing the top of her head. "We've been waiting for you."

* * * * *

KOKOMO

JENNIFER GREENE

From the Author

Dear Reader,

How often have you been driving, flipped on the radio and suddenly heard a song that transported you back in time? The music from our high school years always seems to invoke memories…especially memories of feelings we've never forgotten.

That's why I wrote "Kokomo."

I thought you might like a chance to drift back to a hot summer, back in high school, to remember those yearnings, that hopefulness, those dreams…and yeah, the boys who stirred your imagination back then!

Enjoy…

All my best,

Jennifer Greene

To all the boys we loved before…

CHAPTER 1

Talk about hellishly hot. The idiotic client had the demented idea to have a lunch meeting al fresco. Outside! Connecticut summers were traditionally warm, but it had been over a hundred degrees all week. Not just hot. Mean hot. Blistering, sick hot. Relentless hot.

Jane Whitcomb yanked open the door. The lobby of Bentham, James, Lambrect and Whitcomb was predictably cool, the décor soothing and tasteful, but nothing seemed to appease her cranky mood. She'd cinched the contract with the client—a downright brilliant deal, if she said so herself, and in spite of the sweaty, killer heat—but that didn't seem to lift her spirits, either.

As she clipped down the hall toward her office, young interns ducked from her sight. Those few bodies near the water cooler zoomed back to their offices with heads down. One hapless temp opened the door to the women's restroom, saw Jane, and headed right back into the restroom.

This wasn't the first time she'd noticed the phenomenon, but initially she hadn't connected the behavior with herself. Lately, though, it was hard to avoid realizing that her co-workers' reaction to her had been steadily deteriorating. Jane's feelings were starting to feel bruised. Granted, for the past couple months she'd been in an incessant hurry and stressed to beat the band and tired from the inside out. But people were treating her as if she were…well, as if she were a bitch.

How could the once-most-popular girl in high school, the one they all nicknamed Peachy, the one everyone clamored to be with because she was fun and full of energy and ideas and laughter, possibly have turned into…well, into a bitch?

Whatever. A half mile of pink slips had accumulated by her phone over lunch. The files for the Baker, Spikas, Webster and Bailey contracts were heaped on her blotter. Her appointment calendar claimed she had a conflict—two conflicts—for later that afternoon, and the partners had called an impromptu emergency meeting over an imminent crisis with a client at four that day.

Absently she yanked open the desk drawer and scooped up some antacid tablets from her stock, then grabbed the phone. John—one of the partners—showed up in the doorway with his tie askew, looking frazzled, but she motioned him away. By then she was speed dialing through the problem list.

Halfway through the sixth call…it was the oddest thing…she developed a tic. Her right eye just kept trying to blink, nothing painful or frightening, but unsolvably annoying—and besides that, the last call required information from the Johnson brief.

The Johnson brief should have been on her desk. She shifted through papers and files, then burrowed faster than a woodchuck digging for prey. Pencils flew. Paper clips dropped. Slips of paper and notes floated to the thick, plush blue carpet.

No Johnson brief showed up.

Eyes narrowed, Jane rounded the desk and stormed outside her office, only to see her assistant's desk—temporarily manned by a temp, yet another damn thing going wrong lately—was deserted. Surely this soon after lunch the darn woman couldn't be taking a break already? She zoomed down the hall and slapped open the door to the restroom.

"Marcia? You in here?"

A small voice from one of the locked stalls answered. "Yes, Ms. Whitcomb."

"Where'd you put the Johnson brief?"

"Ma'am…I'm in the bathroom. If you'd just wait for a minute or two—"

Hmmph. She hiked back to the office, and started another frantic search, thinking how the sam hill long could it take the woman to pee?

A strain of an old song filled her mind. She couldn't place it, couldn't remember all the words, but once she got the tune in her head, she couldn't shake it. "Aruba…Jamaica…Key Largo…Montego…"

The phone rang. She grabbed it. Finished that call and handled a second. Still, she rifled through every drawer, then the credenza and desktop for the Johnson brief. "Come on, pretty mama…."

DAMN it. She had to have the brief. Now. Yesterday. Partners were expected to bill seventy hours a week. She'd been billing eighty to eighty-five. Awing them. Awing herself. Only she hadn't had a break since she could remember, and just possibly she had more balls in the air than hands to juggle them. "Kokomo…"

The tic in her eye wouldn't let UP. She jammed the heel of her hand against it, reached for the top shelf over the credenza, knowing perfectly well the brief couldn't possibly be up there— but it couldn't just walk away, either, and it had to be somewhere.

She couldn't reach the top shelf. Being five foot two was the bane of her life. Even three-inch heels didn't add enough height to look imposing, and right now, she was determined to search every inch of the office for the brief—no matter what it took.

She kicked off her heels, hiked up her skirt and climbed on top of her desk…which was when she noticed the temp standing in the doorway. Marcia was one of those women who somehow always managed to look vulnerable. She had mouse-brown hair, puppy-dog eyes and had the build of a cookie addict—plump and soft. At the moment she stood motionless, with an expression that looked as if she could start shaking any second.

"I was just…" Jane started to say, but then caught herself. Maybe it was the horror and fear in the temp's eyes, but she suddenly saw herself as the young woman seemed to be seeing her. Standing on top of her desk. The office in shambles. Paper and files everywhere. A cup overturned. Four lights blinking simultaneously on the phone. Her private fax was vomiting page after page in a bulimic fit, and the couch where clients were supposed to be able to sit was completely covered in paper and fallout debris.

Jane found herself gulping. This was just never how she'd expected to behave as a lawyer.

This was never how she'd expected her work or her private life to turn out, either.

And suddenly something snapped inside her.

Slowly she climbed down from the desk. Even more slowly, she sank into her office chair. "Marcia," she said.

"Yes, Ms. Whitcomb."

"I need a break."

"Yes. You do. The whole office thinks you do."

"I haven't taken a vacation in three years." Now that that infamous "something" had snapped, it was like a hem on a skirt. Once the thread got loose, the whole thing unraveled. She knuckled her eyes for a moment, a little scared—as ridiculous as it sounded—that she just might cave in and cry. Then, of course, she pulled it back together. "I would appreciate it if you would get me plane tickets. For…"

The where-of-it was the major question, since she had absolutely no destination in mind. But then that song came back into her head, as if fate were just waiting to help her out that afternoon. "Kokomo. Round trip tickets to Kokomo. I want eight straight days. Set up the first and last nights in a hotel near the airport. I'll take care of the rest myself when I get there."

"Kokomo," Marcia said carefully. "Are you sure?"

"I am *dead* sure. In fact, I don't think I've been this sure of anything since…" Who knew since when? Since she'd firs. heard that song a zillion summers ago. Since *that* long.

"But, Ms. Whitcomb— '

"Now. I want it done now. Just make the reservations on the soonest possible flight. Let me know the time. I don't want to hear another word about it."

"But Ms. Whitcomb—"

"Not another word. I mean it. I'm going to shut down my client projects, get things shifted and delegated so I can leave. But if there's a prayer in the universe of being on a plane to Kokomo by tomorrow, I want to be on it."

"Ms. Whitcomb, are you absolutely certain that—"

"Marcia." There now. Once she used that certain tone of voice, the temp shut up, nodded quickly and scurried out of sight.

Unfortunately, Jane realized she'd been a bitch again. It didn't make her feel good. Maybe there wasn't a justifiable excuse for behaving like a perimenopausal Wicked Witch of the West, but there actually was a reason.

She was miserable.

Who knew?

People not only avoided her; they'd been acting downright afraid of her. You'd think she might have picked up a few clues that people didn't want to be anywhere around her if they could help it. But that was precisely the kicker.

She hadn't noticed at all. She'd been running so fast, for so long, that she not only hadn't stopped to smell the roses. She hadn't stopped long enough to realize she'd turned into a miserably unhappy sharp thorn.

WHEN JANE BOARDED the plane, her eyes were only open to half slits and she wasn't speaking—to anyone. Five in the morning wasn't her best hour. Because it had taken most of the night to prepare for being gone, she'd barely caught a couple hours of sleep. She hadn't even opened a suitcase until past two in the morning, but at least at that point, realized that packing didn't matter. She tossed some cosmetics and swimwear and shorts in a single bag and called it quits, knowing she could shop when she got there.

Now she stumbled down the narrow aisle, found her seat, hurled her purse down and strapped in. She didn't know how long the flight was. Didn't care. She'd only glanced at her e-ticket to know the flight time, and had ignored the rest of the arrangements Marcia had made just as happily. None of the details mattered now. The flight to Kokomo was surely long enough to catch several hours of sleep, and with a hotel pre-set up for the first night, she could catch even more. After that she had to do some thinking and planning, but not before.

The faces she passed vaguely registered. It wasn't a huge jet. The back of the plane was already filled, most of the passengers already tucked down and snoozing. But she passed a skinny businessman, a nerdy kid with a blond afro, a handsome guy in a military uniform, two teenage girls babbling to each other...when she finally located her seat, she thanked the travel gods for the empty seat next to her, but also noticed two white-haired women in the seats across, both heavy set, who looked to be sound asleep.

She couldn't wait to do the same. She fixed a pillow behind her neck just so, sighed, and closed her eyes.

They popped back open. *Wide* open.

No one as exhausted as she was—days exhausted, weeks exhausted, MONTHS exhausted—could possibly have trouble sleeping.

Or so she told herself. Yet when she tried squeezing her eyes closed again, the lids jerked up faster than a jack-in-the-box.

As the jet engines revved for takeoff, in fact, she found her gaze fixed on the passenger three rows ahead.

She'd already noticed him. It was the good-looking guy in the military uniform, the one in the aisle of the emergency seat…she could see his long legs stretched out, see a wedge of his dark hair in profile, and even from here, she caught the shine of brass on the arm of his uniform. Still, those physical details weren't what snared her attention. There'd been something when she'd passed him….a flash in his dark eyes, something in his angular profile, the chin…that now struck her with a slap of recognition, as if she knew him.

She couldn't place a single person she knew in uniform— much less one who'd earned all that brass. She had to have imagined it…or maybe her pulse kicked her awake for a more obvious reason. He was one helluva good-looking guy.

It wasn't as if it mattered. In a thousand years she wouldn't give a stranger any serious thought…but that didn't mean she was blind. He was definitely riveting enough to put some zest in a girl's heartbeat.

In her case, though, Jane wasn't dead sure if zest was a precise definition for the physical symptoms she was suffering. She forgot the guy and slammed her eyes closed again, all too aware that her heart was pounding. So was her pulse. And her temple.

It seemed as if that pounding had become a consuming way of life, like being miserable and mean and bitchy.

The only new symptom was fear. Something seemed to be very, very wrong with her. The last time she remembered putting herself through any serious self-analysis, she'd been a teenager—a bright, happy, driven teenager who'd known exactly what she wanted in life, gone after it, fought for it, and won it.

So how could she possibly be so unhappy when she had every darn thing she'd ever wanted?

Trying to relax, she forced her mind to concentrate on the Count The Blessing thing. Heaven knew, that took a while, because she really had a ton of them. When push came down to shove, she couldn't think of a single thing to complain about.

Her divorce was three years old—old enough for all the sharp edges to have faded. Cray had never cheated on her, never been abusive. He'd just been a parasite, the kind of guy who picked an ambitious wife so he could loll around and live off her earnings. Maybe she could have tolerated that longer if he'd just loved her—but whatever. The point was that she was happily single, and still downright thrilled to be free from Cray.

The kids were all doing fabulous—Bry married and spending a year in Alaska with his bride, Lar career-launched in Seattle and her baby was still home—Angel—but spending the summer on an exchange program in Europe before starting her senior year in college.

Her house was paid for. Her new white Lexus a love. Her closets filled with Elie Tahari and St. John's. And shoes. God knew, she had a weakness for shoes. All of it was paid for, though, and she'd earned every dime—had a lucrative, successful career. Lots of respect. She'd never wanted to be mediocre—she'd wanted to be an outstanding contract lawyer or nothing—and she'd met that goal, too.

She nestled her behind in the seat, determined to get more

comfortable. The more blessings she counted, the more obvious it became. She was happy. She *had* to be happy.

So why in the Sam Hill was there salty moisture jammed up under her closed eyes?

When she got to that damned Caribbean island, Jane told herself, she was going to kick herself but good. And that old summer song suddenly strolled into her mind again. Soothing her. Easing away all that stress. "That's where I want to go…down to Kokomo…"

It was a minute later…no more. She positively hadn't slept a wink. Not a single one.

Yet she was suddenly startled to hear a young girl's voice rise in a scream of fear.

Instead of bright morning light pouring in the port windows, it was darker than pitch outside, and the plane seemed to be pitching, as well. Another female voice cried out.

The pilot's voice came on the loudspeaker, his tone calm but terse.

"I know the turbulence is unpleasant, but please stay calm. As soon as we're on the ground, as fast as we can exit you all from the plane, we'll be aiming straight for a protected area. I understand that you'll be concerned about your luggage and your plans, but there will be no flights out of the Kokomo area until these storms have passed. We can't outrun these storms, folks, so just stay calm, and we'll be on the ground as fast as we can get you there…."

Jane heard him, but her attention was abruptly ransomed by the view outside her window. From a thick clot of smoky-black clouds, a funnel suddenly shot downward. Then a second funnel. When the jet turned to approach the runaway, a passenger on the other side of the aisle shrieked, "Tornadoes! We're all going to die! Can you see the tornadoes?"

But then another voice intervened. A man's voice, saying, "It's going to be all right. We'll be on the ground in less than a minute now. We're all going to be fine."

That voice…it was crazy, but Jane knew that voice.

Danger electrified the air in the cabin. It was hard to make sense of anything in the next few minutes—the crazy darkness. What time it was. Where they were. The storms had shown up from a crystal-clear sky as if from nowhere. The jet bounced on the tarmac, the brakes screeching no louder than everyone's heartbeats. Jane could taste fear at the back of her throat. Not the kind of fear she associated with stress and pressure, but the other kind. The *real* kind.

Yet that man's voice kept echoing in her mind, buttercoating her nerves, soothing her. She just…believed that voice. Believed what he said about being fine. Some instinct kept reassuring her that she knew the voice, knew the man speaking, knew she could trust him.

The elderly man across the aisle suddenly looked right at her. "Where are we, do you know?" Jane asked.

"Kokomo," he responded. "And it seems like we're going to make it there by the skin of our teeth."

But when Jane looked out, past the black clouds and the tumultuous wind and deluge of a rain…she saw no sign of a tropical paradise. The view revealed a flat landscape, backdropped by the buildings of a middle-sized ordinary American town, with farm country visible in the far distance.

Naturally if they needed to make an emergency landing, it didn't matter where they were. But she was confused by the other passenger's response.

"This can't be Kokomo," she said.

The man raised one shaggy white eyebrow. "I promise you, it is. I was born in Kokomo, Indiana. I should know."

Kokomo, *Indiana?* Jane stared at the man in complete bewilderment—but a second later, the jet slammed to a stop and the passengers hustled toward the doors in a fury of frantic pandemonium.

CHAPTER 2

Jane couldn't possibly consider panicking, simply because everyone else was. The doors to the plane hadn't been opened yet, but people were too freaked to stay in their seats. The pilot and co-pilot swiftly emerged from the cockpit and tried to urge calm and quiet. And the man—the one in the uniform, the delicious one that Jane kept thinking she knew—emerged as another natural take-charge person.

The flight attendant would undoubtedly normally be of more help, but the girl looked young, as untried and scared as the passengers. "It's just unbelievable. There were a few rainstorms in the forecast, but nothing like this system, no threat of tornadoes or wind like this. The whole thing seemed to show up out of nowhere…."

"This way, people. Straight down the stairs and toward the open door. There's an attendant there…."

The older man in front of Jane stumbled. She grabbed his arm. The two teenagers up front were still shrieking and crying.

The uniformed man—*her* man—kept offering quiet, sensible advice. "Take your purse or bag, make sure you've got whatever medications or critical items you were carrying with you. Nothing else. We can worry about everything else later.

At the bottom of the stairs, walk with someone else. Prepare for the wind. That's it, that's it…"

When Jane reached him, it wasn't a thunderbolt from the tornado that hit her, but a different kind of thunderbolt entirely.

She *did* know him.

"You need help?" he asked her when she paused at the door.

"No, no, I'm fine!" It was no time to act like a blundering fool. If he recognized her, he didn't let on. But memories suddenly rushed at her with the force of a battering ram.

Henry White. That's who he was. Hank. Her Hank—once upon a time. Once upon a long, long ago time.

At the doorway to the plane the wind snarled around her, grabbing at her shirt, her hair, rain pummeling her with wild, sharp pellets. She was completely soaked in seconds, and gasped for air, yet there seemed nothing to breathe but that choking thick wind. Crazy things hurled through the air— chair legs and towels, pieces of metal and shreds of paper, branches when there wasn't a tree in sight. The howl of the storm made hearing any conversation impossible. Something stabbed her arm, stung. It was all she could do to hold the handrail and get down the stairs.

Someone gasped behind her—two women, both her mother's age—and because they were struggling just to stay on their feet, she reached for both of them.

The three ran toward the open door of the airport terminal. Just negotiating those thirty yards seemed more challenging and exhausting than running miles.

"Come on, come on, come on!" A uniformed airport staff person brusquely grabbed at them, pulled them in, shoved them toward the right. "There. Keep going. Past the windows, past the revolving door. Then sit on the ground against the concrete wall. Hurry, everyone! Hurry, hurry!"

She heard it. The sounds outside changed. Suddenly it was more than storm, more than rain, but wind spiraling into a weapon. She did what everyone else did. Hurtled toward safety, packing close to everyone else, huddling down against the cold cement wall. She wrapped her arms around her knees and ducked her head.

People were crying. Men, women, made no difference. The whole corridor and terminal and anterooms were dim-dark—clearly they'd lost power. Yet even inside, protected by cement walls, Jane could hear the roar of wind, the menace of it.

She saw a dark shadow hustle into the area where they were, heard someone say, "My God, it hit the plane," and then none of them said or did anything. Just sat there, huddled and chilled and afraid. Waiting.

Vaguely she recognized that her left arm had a pretty good scrape, because blood had soaked through her salmon silk shirt.

And she was starting to feel chilled to the bone, whether from fear or being rain-soaked—or both. She always wore her hair short and neat, because there was no other way to control the thick curls, but now her hair was all tangled and wet, too. Her pants, a silk twill, clung stickily to her thighs and butt.

Still, she was no more miserable than anyone else, and right then it kept hitting her: they were alive. Being alive hadn't struck her as amazing three hours ago, but it sure as hell did now. From moment to moment, her mind kept trying to wrap around being in Kokomo, *Indiana*—**how** in the universe could she have ended up here? Yet she remembered Marcia repeatedly asking her, are you sure, are you *sure*?...so she could all too easily piece together how this had happened.

Marcia hadn't believed she really meant Kokomo, Indiana, but Jane—being the bitch she'd turned into lately—hadn't really given the temp a chance to clarify her question. Or what she wanted.

And now none of that mattered anyway.

A tornado seemed to be an amazing equalizer.

So much of an equalizer that the only clear thought that kept surfacing in her head was Hank. Hank White.

It just struck her as crazily ironic. If she *had* to land in the middle of a tornado, she just wished it could be with a man she hadn't jilted in high school. A boy she'd once hurt as blithely as squashing a mosquito. A boy she'd treated very, very badly.

A boy who'd done nothing but love her, once upon a time.

She was still thinking about that, thinking about the summer of her senior year, the summer when she'd still believed in endless possibilities and "once upon a times," when the heartthrob of her old daydreams suddenly showed up in front of her.

He hunkered down, as if seeking to speak quietly without the rest of the passengers overhearing. But he clearly didn't recognize her. He just said, "My name's Henry White. Hank. You up for doing a little work? We could use a little organization and help."

"Sure," she said immediately, and pushed to her feet.

She wasn't the only one he'd picked. Another four passengers were quietly isolated from the pack—all men—and shown into a narrow back office. Their pilot, a pilot from another plane and several frazzled airport personnel were already there. Hank, though, was the one who spoke up.

"We're not facing an easy day ahead, as I'm sure you all already guessed. Tornadoes ripped through this whole area. We have no power here, beyond an emergency generator, and it's possible local hospitals or emergency services could need that more than we do. There are live wires all through the city of Kokomo and surrounding roads. Downed lines and trees and buildings are blocking the roads and tarmacs…"

He looked right at her, but no differently than he made eye contact with everyone else in the room. Jane kept thinking, surely she hadn't changed that much; he'd recognize her any second…yet he didn't seem to.

She, on the other hand, could hardly keep her eyes off him. He'd been an adorable boy. Shy and quiet, but still, he had that strong bone structure, the height, the sharp intelligence in his eyes that all set him apart. The dark eyes were downright dreamy—then and now. The shock of dark hair was extra striking next to his Irish-clear skin.

"At least there has only been our flight and one other that were stranded here. They were in the same boat that we were. No opportunity to divert to another airfield in time. The storms came up too fast, too unexpectedly. The point, though, is that we're all stranded here. We're not sure for how long, but our best guess is two or three days."

The others expressed sounds of dismay. Jane might have felt the same dismay…but she still couldn't take her eyes off Hank.

"We're safe," he said. "That's the good news. And frankly,

it's damned good news. Those were hellacious storms. But the bad news is…things are going to get messy here."

"So what do we do to help?" Jane asked immediately.

Again, his gaze honed on her, still not with recognition—other than that he'd seemed to naturally isolate her, with some instinct that she'd keep a level head in a crisis.

"We need water. Food. Sanitation—the bathrooms are going to get rank damn fast if we can't flush. And we don't have shower facilities or spare water for washing. We'll also need sleeping arrangements. Someone to liaise with the passengers to make sure no one needs special medicine or care. The plane was damaged. But we'll be able to get luggage out, get people's things for a few days…nobody's going to be happy, but we should be able to cope well enough if we just organize and come together…."

Two male passengers wearing suits were given the assignment of unloading luggage, blankets and pillows from the plane now that the wind had died down. The group talked about setting up staging areas, so belongings didn't get spread out all through the airport, and ways to address issues of security and privacy.

The airport staff and co-pilot got into a major discussion about sanitation. One of the passengers was an engineer, and already started rolling up his sleeves.

Jane opened her mouth several times to volunteer, but in the first round of acknowledged problems, everybody else seemed to sweep in ahead of her with some level of knowledge or expertise she didn't have. She had to admit, creating a soup kitchen or temporary latrines wasn't in any job description she'd ever had.

Still, everybody seemed to have a chore and major responsibility except for her. And as each person or pair hustled out to address their projects, suddenly there seemed no way left in the shadowy room but her and Hank.

"You didn't give me a job."

He leaned against a desk. "Actually, I left you the most critical one. Your name?"

"Jane," she said. "Jane Whitcomb." Instinctively she braced, because the instant she said her name, she thought it would click for him.

He'd remember her dumping him, what a heartless creep she'd been. And maybe she deserved his looking at her as if she were a worm in his past...but it was so odd. Because she wasn't remembering her rotten behavior half as much as she was suddenly recalling other parts of that long, hot summer. Like...his laying her up against the high school brick wall and kissing her senseless.

Like...his lying next to her at the beach, both of them beaded with water under a hot sun, her pretending to nap but really fascinated by the rock-hard erection he kept trying to hide, her feeling sky-high powerful as a woman.

Like...the summer cotillion dance. The one where she'd worn a white strapless gown, long and silky. The one where the orchestra had started out playing traditional waltzes, but past ten, when most of the country club parents had started fading from sight and gone home, the musicians had loosened up and played some classic rock and roll. She didn't remember the songs, except for one. The Beach Boys one. The Kokomo one.

She'd been so happy that night, so high being with Hank...yet it wasn't Hank she'd gone home with.

It wasn't Hank she'd slept with.

It was another boy. Not a boy she loved. A boy she thought at the time—believed at the time—was her future.

"Are you with me so far, Jane?"

Swiftly she mentally slapped herself. "I'm sorry. I missed some of what you said. It's been such a stressful morning—"

"That's all right. But you really are the only one I think could do this well. We need to help people stay calm, not panic. We need someone to find out if there is anyone with special diet or health needs that should be addressed. We've got doers, but we don't have an assigned 'people person.' I think the flight attendant might normally do that job, but if you met her—"

"I understand."

"No one would listen to her. So it would really help if you could…" Suddenly he hesitated, and shook his head with a boyish laugh. "You're going to think this is crazy, but I keep getting the weirdest feeling that I've met you before."

She opened her mouth to respond, yet only a gulp emerged. Of course she was going to admit who she was, that they'd known each other before. Only…it suddenly wasn't that easy.

She didn't want him to hate her. Didn't want him to remember what she'd done.

Maybe more so, because in these past few days, she was coming to realize—with a whole lot of pain—that she was still that girl. Only aged. Not like wine, where age made it better. But more like champagne, where the grapes that once looked and tasted stupendous started to sour with time.

Not that she was sour, exactly. But…

She was.

Sour. On the inside.

But Hank was standing there—in the middle of a crisis, for Pete's sake—stuck waiting for an answer.

"You know me," she admitted. "We knew each other—"

But the pilot—Captain Bunker—abruptly popped his head in. "Hank, if you could come out here for a minute—"

"Sure, right away." And he was gone—but not before flashing her a swift, curious smile. "We'll catch up later."

She didn't see him again for ages. When everyone had gotten off the plane, gotten to safety, they'd all been quiet—fear-quiet—through the storms. But now the tornadoes were over, or everyone believed they were, and the terminal had turned into complete chaos. People wanted to go outside. Wanted food. Wanted to phone families and businesses. Wanted their luggage, their cars, their connections. Wanted to know what was going to happen next. When. How. Where. Why.

There were plenty of uniforms running around—whether they were airport staff or pilots or, like Hank, just a natural leader because of his military rank—so Jane found it bewildering how many hands plucked at her sleeve, chased after to ask her questions. But she suddenly got it, why Hank had pulled her from the crowd.

It was the female thing. The older women and kids especially wanted to ask a female, wanted female-type reassurance. And especially the women wanted answers to pressing personal problems.

"My sister..." The two white-haired ladies from the first row of first class looked like mirror-twins. "...has diabetes. And she had insulin in her purse. But now we don't know where her purse is. We think she left it on the plane, but now nobody will let us go back to the plane to look…."

"Okay," Jane said. "I'll get it. What's the purse look like? And do you need food right now?"

Then there was an old man on spindly legs, Walter, who pulled on her wrist. "Miss. My sister died. I'm here for the funeral. I need to go home."

"I understand. But I gather it's really dangerous out there, sir. Live electric wires in the roads. Big chunks of debris strewn on the road and runways. So for a while, the safest place we can be is right here. And whoever's in your family…they know. If they live locally, they just went through the same storms…and if they live close, they've heard about the tornadoes on the news. So they'll be worried, for sure, but we'll get you out of here just as soon as we can."

As she reached the door, it was the teenaged girls who ran her down. Neither were looking so perky now; they both had mascara running down their cheeks. "We need a bathroom."

"They're going to set up some kind of sanitation facilities as fast as they can. I'm guessing you can use the women's room to pee. But I don't know if or when we'll have some generator power, so for right now I'm guessing we just don't have water to flush or wash our hands."

"But I have to wash my face—"

"The only water we're going to use for a stretch here, is for drinking or food. I'm hoping that won't be for long—" She could see the girls were about to argue further, and decided she'd better come up with a diversion pronto. "I could really use your help, if you two wouldn't mind.

"Like," Jane said, "first just see if you can scout out the whole terminal facility for me. Check out the upstairs, see if there are any big rooms up there. If we're stuck for a couple of nights we might want to set up some privacy areas for men and women. Or just find out what the layout is like, okay?"

"Can we go behind the desks, even places like that?" Both girls showed an immediate trigger of interest.

"You mean the private offices? Well…I think as long as you're on a reconnaissance mission like this, it'll be okay. If someone questions you, just tell them that Jane asked you to do this job."

"Hey, that's cool."

Then there was an older man, Ronald, who hobbled over with a walker to gravely state that he'd been in two wars and three international conflicts, and what could he do to help?

He looked so frail that she couldn't imagine anything physical he could do, but she saw how clear and sharp his eyes were. How proud.

And slowly she said, "It would really, really help if you'd set up where you could see the front doors. We've been all asked to stay inside for a while, to make sure where everyone is, that all the passengers are accounted for. And I guess, to make sure no one goes out until the storm's damage has been determined. But I don't think there's any way everyone's going to obey that. The smokers will be sneaking out, for sure. But people are also curious, want to see what's going on, want the fresh air. So…if you could just station yourself by the doors? Take note if someone leaves the building and let one of guys in uniform know? Or me. I'll check back with you in a little while."

He gave her a thumbs up. "I'm your man."

And that was when the thought clicked in her head. People were understandably frustrated and upset—but they would tend to panic less if everyone had something to *do*.

God knows she had a gift for being bossy. Might as well put it to use.

Hours later she was light-headed from lack of food; her Italian silk slacks were ruined, her feet were killing her and the scrape on her arm was angrily stinging. As she stole out a back door for a few seconds' break, though, she felt oddly exhilarated.

She hadn't thought of the office in hours. Hadn't been this long without a computer or phone since she could remember. And all the passengers, no matter how upset, seemed to assume she was a capable, warmhearted woman—instead of the Bitch Times Three she'd turned into lately.

It was a long way from the Caribbean vacation she had in mind or desperately needed.

But she had the odd sensation of climbing in someone else's skin for a while. She had no idea whose—but it definitely wasn't her own. She got to be someone else today, and no one ever had to know otherwise.

She pushed open the farthest back door, the one that usually led passengers out to private flights. She expected no one would have any reason to be there, and she could catch a moment's privacy. Instead, the view stunned her into immediate silence.

The air was still hot, still humid, still choked with that

electric smell warning of storms. The sky had all the blue leached from it, the color swirling with gray and yellow clouds, a moody wind still chasing debris in all directions.

On one runway, an orange truck sat on top of a white SUV. A hundred yards farther, a tree just lay on the blacktop…a huge, old tree with giant gnarly roots…even though there wasn't a forest or woods in sight. Part of a roof blocked a hangar. Garbage and paper and plastic and every other kind of trash looked as if a fairy-tale ogre had spilled massive messes from his garbage truck.

Now she got it. Why everyone had been urged to stay inside, why no one was likely to be traveling anywhere for hours, if not days. If the whole town was in as bad a shape as the airport, heaven knew how long it would take it clear it all.

Their plane didn't look exactly bad—assuming the hole it had put in the building wasn't too catastrophic. She could see the belly, where luggage was stored, almost emptied now and brought into the building. And then she noticed the fire.

At first she couldn't make sense of it, but then she had to smile. It looked as if five home gas barbecues had been nestled together to create a giant cook space. Judging from the pots and food, it appeared as if individual families—or restaurants—had emptied out their freezers, and rather than lose food because of the power outage, had simply contributed to a massive cooking effort. Heaven knew what the result would be. Or how long they would be eating whatever had gone into those big, fat pots. But they definitely weren't going to starve. The two plump ladies who'd sat in the first aisle looked as if they were in their glory, huge spoons in their hands, their pink cheeks double-flushed from their cooking.

"Peachy."

She whirled around, for the first time realizing that Hank had been outside, too, leaned against the building in the shade. He'd lost his military jacket, but not the bearing. Everything about him was hopelessly male. He'd so clearly grown into a guy comfortable in his own skin. A guy who'd become a leader, who didn't have to shout anything about his gender or his job or the success he'd made of his life. It was all there, in his clear dark eyes, his posture, the way he took in the world.

The way he looked at her.

And abruptly, she heard the "Peachy."

"You remembered," she said.

"I think I knew you the minute I laid eyes on you. But with the tornadoes—all this chaos—any connection just went to the back of my mind." He cocked his head, studying her. "Your hair's shorter. But otherwise you look the same."

"That's it. You're my hero forever." She told herself to smile, then realized she already was. "I wasn't sure if I wanted you to remember me. I'm pretty unhappy at the way I treated you years ago."

His eyebrows lifted. "All I remember is a great senior summer. And isn't this crazy? To meet up after all these years in a Kokomo, Indiana airport? Of all the places in the universe?"

"Beyond crazy—how do you happen to be here?"

"Grissom Air Force Base is a hop and jump from here. I have an old friend getting a promotion, flew in on the q.t. to be there for him. Or that was the plan. How about you?"

She started to answer, but his previous comment was still glued in her mind. All those summers ago, she'd hurt him badly, she knew. Yet now it so obviously didn't matter to him. He'd clearly made so much of his life that any memories of her were only a minor blip on his radar screen.

And that was a big thank heavens, she told herself. If the past didn't bother him, there was no reason to feel awkward. Or to carry around any more guilt. But...

It startled her.

That she was the one, that long-ago summer, who'd known exactly what she wanted from life. She'd pinned down a career, personal goals and needs, labeled the whole kind of future she wanted in every way.

Hank only had one goal that summer. To be with her.

Yet he was the one who looked happy now.

And she was the one hoping they'd be stranded with tornado weather just a little while longer so she didn't have to go back to her "wonderful" life.

CHAPTER 3

"But Jane. I don't understand why Joella gets a bed and I don't."

"There are only three cots in the whole building, Delores. The rest of us are lucky just to have carpet and blankets."

"But Joella only has arthritis. I'm a cancer survivor. And I have diabetes. I'm suffering a whole lot more than she is. On top of which, I think she took my hiddenite."

"Hiddenite?"

"Yes. You know about chakras, don't you? Well, I paid a lot for that mineral. And I was lying on the cot—just borrowing the cot for a while this afternoon, mind you, and it was after they delivered the luggage…"

"Uh-huh…"

"So I'd gotten out my hiddenite. Now there's only one way to use it right, I don't care what anybody says. You have to lie on your back and put the hiddenite stone right in the middle of your chest. It creates a feeling of harmony. But like I told my cousin Louise, I said, Louise, it's also very good for helping with heart palpitations. Only, next thing, I open my eyes and it's gone. I know Joella took it. I know. Because she always did want whatever I had… She's jealous of me. That's what. Always has been—"

The intrepid Delores had followed her from one end of the building to the other. Tarps had been used to create makeshift curtains, allowing for some basic privacy between the genders. Jane had been running all day—as had everyone, she knew—hustling to make sleeping arrangements before they lost all natural light. It was nine now. Late enough. The accommodations weren't fancy, but between airline blankets and pillows, and the clothes people had packed in their suitcases, everyone had something to use as a pillow and a way to keep warm.

"Jane!"

One of the teenagers, the one with the pearl in her eyebrow, who was on the third change of clothes since getting her suitcase, accosted her before Delores had finished.

"Rina told me we couldn't use toilet paper."

Ah. All day long, said Rina had been spreading rumors, helping a certain group stay riled up ALL the time. "This is the thing, honey. We can't have normal sanitation when we're so limited on fresh water. So if we throw toilet paper in the toilets, it'll clog the system when we do get power back."

"But I have to use toilet paper."

Jane nodded. "And that's fine. But throw the toilet paper in the black plastic container in the restroom."

"You mean, in front of everybody?"

"Honey. We're all in the same boat. No one likes it."

"But it's so unclean and gross and embarrassing—"

"Uh-huh. For everyone. But at least we've got dry hand cleaner for everyone. I know it's a wild thought, but maybe you could skip using makeup just for these couple of days."

The sixteen-year-old looked at her as if she'd suggested walking naked down the street.

"Jane, you haven't answered *my* problem about the cot." Delores plucked at her sleeve again.

The blond man who'd sat at the back of the plane hailed her from across the room. "I've been trying to track you down, Jane." That morning, Dwight had had the look of a businessman, but he'd long lost the tie, added a day's stubble to his chin, and had mighty tired eyes.

"I know," she said gently. "You're terribly worried about your wife. I don't blame you." There were no functioning landlines, no way to plug in cell phones or laptop computers. The staff had gotten a generator going, but emergency needs had already taxed it to the limit—all of which Dwight knew. "I talked to the captain and to the airport staff. They're certain either police or National Guard will get in here by early tomorrow. The thing is, the whole city was hit so hard that we're just not a priority."

"I understand that. It's just….my Sara's pregnant—"

"And you're worried like hell." Jane squeezed his shoulder, swiftly, warmly, then let him go. "I would be, too. But I'm sure your wife's heard on the state and national news by now that we're okay. So there's every chance she knows where you are, and that you just can't temporarily reach her. And when we get some help in here tomorrow, we'll have a way to get messages out. You're at the top of that list. I promise you won't be forgotten."

Delores was still trailing after her. "Jane," she said. "What about my cot?"

Well, she couldn't very well put off the lady any longer. She motioned her into the alcove that held the now-nonfunctional game and pop machines. An ideal place for a private conversation. "Delores," she said gently, "I think it's terrible, just terrible, that your friend Joella would take one of the few cots when you're suffering so much. But I think, ideally, what you could do is create a bed for yourself with clothes—bunching up soft spots and support exactly where you want it. A cot is just…hard. If you use clothes and pillows and soft jackets and all, you're going to have a much, much softer bed than your friend. Not that I'd tell her that."

"Oh, I won't," Delores assured her. She hesitated, but then remembered, "But what about the hiddenite she stole from me?"

"Now that's a very serious thing," she said gravely, thankful she'd had a couple neighbors who'd relentlessly enthused about certain new-age ideas. Possibly Delores had mangled the philosophical concepts to suit herself, but at least Jane understood the gist of the older woman's complaint. "But I don't think we'd want anyone else to hear about that hiddenite, would we? Because probably everybody'd want to steal it then."

"Oh! I didn't think of that! You're so right!"

"And if I know my chakras…and I do," Jane assured her.

"You do?"

"Oh, yes! So I know that the power of the stone will wear out unless it's cleansed and, um, discharged once a week in a bowl of sea salt."

Delores's jaw dropped. "You *do* know!"

"Doesn't everyone?" Jane added in a whisper, "The point is, that anyone who stole it would only get value from the mineral for a really short time. After that, there's no reason she shouldn't give it back to you. And once you discharge it, then it'll work for you again. Right?"

"Jane, Jane, Jane…you're one outstanding woman. Not like some of the riffraff on that plane."

"Thank you, Delores. I really appreciate…" From the corner of her eye, she saw Hank barely two yards away, hands on hips, rolling his eyes at her. "…your vote of support. I need to help Colonel White with something now, okay?"

"Certainly, dear, certainly…."

When the plump little lady wandered off, she faced Hank—who seemed to be crooking his finger at her. Apparently he'd overheard the conversation and seemed to think she'd suddenly turned into a lunatic.

"Look, you gave me the job of handling complaints! I'm trying to keep some of the trickier passengers off your back! I'm doing the best I can!"

Still, he motioned her closer.

"Okay, so I can't say I believe in magical minerals and mysticism and all, but I had to tell her something. Most of the passengers are terrific. They're all stepping up to be helpful. There are just a few who seem to be on the pain-in-the-keester high maintenance list. I—"

Her voice failed her when he grabbed her hand. It wasn't as if she minded if he touched her. It was just…a surprise. The sudden warmth and zing of connection. The way he slid his fingers between hers, the way teenagers held hands or at least the way *they'd* held hands back when. At the time, holding hands had seemed corny—even if she liked it—and now, well, he seemed to be herding her past the ticket counter toward a private door.

He glanced around, as if to insure no one was looking, and then quickly opened the door and ushered her inside.

"I think," he said, "that you've more than earned combat pay. But since that isn't an option in these circumstances, the crew thought you'd earned a drink."

She blinked when she regarded the reprobates in the back office. Only dim twilight filtered through the long oblong window overlooking the tarmac. With drinking water at a premium, clearly the group was trying not to waste it. In fact, from the concentrated alcoholic fumes in the small space, everyone had to be drinking straight from either mini-airline bottles or their own private stash.

No one was exactly partying. It was just all the spiffy uniforms of the staff that morning had suffered major wrinkles, along with the bodies wearing them. The group was sprawled on the floor under the window, looking exhausted…but good-humored.

"We're all alive," the co-pilot from the second stranded plane—George, she'd come to know—piped up by way of an excuse. "We thought we needed to celebrate that. On top of which, everybody put in a lion's effort today, and we'll all have to turn around and do the same tomorrow. So the consensus was that we should take five to click glasses together. Or paper cups, as it were. Jane—you've done more than your share."

"So has everyone," she said.

"What's your poison?" Hank asked.

"What's available?"

"Almost everything. As long as you don't want water with it or necessarily want more than an ounce at a time."

She laughed. "Scotch, then."

"Scotch? The girl has to have some Irish blood in her some-where," Hank told the group approvingly.

Someone had lit a utility candle, plunked it in a glass on the desk. It flickered a pale light, not enough to illuminate the handful of faces or the room…but it reminded Jane of camp-fires from when she was a girl, the shine of eyes and glow of cheeks in the darkness, the sense of belonging. When Hank handed her the Dixie cup of Scotch, she raised it to salute the group and then took a healthy sip.

It was bad Scotch. Ultra bad. So bad it burned holes in the back of her throat, yet for the first time in—weeks? months?—she felt herself relaxing. She eased down to the floor, cross-legged, inhaling the scents of the candle and heat and alcohol. The scents were hardly an aromatic perfume, but somehow, she associated the mix instinctively with safety.

It was like the co-pilot said. No matter how inconvenient or uncomfortable or frustrated they may be…they were alive. And coping pretty darn well together, at least so far.

Jane realized Hank had plunked down next to her. The others were talking, desultory fashion, about what they were missing. The pilot had been en route to a month's vacation. Two more days of flying and he'd have been in Alaska, his favorite getaway spot. He loved it all, the bears and salmon and eagles and kayaking waters with whales.

Another man spoke up—a staff person from the airport, although Jane didn't know his name. His four-year-old was having a birthday tomorrow. A daughter. He called her Bubble Face. He'd promised to be there, and his wife… "Man, if my wife has to survive eleven four-year-olds on her own, she'll never let me hear the end of it. And Bubble Face, she's been talking about it for weeks. What she's gonna wear. Whether she can have purple frosting on her cake. Whether she's going to get this certain doll. How she gets to put this sparkly stuff on her fingers for the party. On and on."

Jane eased her back against an old-fashioned metal desk. The metal was unyielding, but still felt cool, and just having that physical support against her spine relaxed her nerves another notch. She took another sip, felt Hank glance at her.

She didn't look at him, though, but at the person in the corner who was taking his turn talking. The co-pilot from their plane, who she'd talked to a dozen times that day. He looked a little too GQ to be military, but he was a good-looking guy, and talked and walked like he knew it. Still, he'd chipped in with humor and elbow grease just like everyone else all day.

And now he piped up, "You all sound like you had great stuff to go home to. But frankly, I don't mind being here. I just broke up with a woman I'd been seeing for almost two years. Really didn't want to go home. Still don't. I'm relieved as hell we're all okay—flying into that storm was no fun—and the forecasters should be horsewhipped, if you ask me. But there's nobody I'd rather fly with than Chuck. And so far I don't mind seeing this all as an adventure."

After that, it was Hank's turn at the conversational bat. A déjà vu sensation hit Jane when she saw how he suddenly ducked his head—it was a gesture he'd had, that long ago summer, when he was forced to talk about himself. He'd been an ace in the debate team, could speak in front of a group in high school. That never seemed his worry. He'd just never liked to draw attention to himself personally.

Still, he was game to answer how he'd come to be here and what the tornado had interrupted for him. "I was headed to Griffin Air Force base, to share in a promotion and celebration for an old friend. I grew up in Connecticut, but my home base has been Colorado Springs for years now. The Air Force Academy is there. Pikes Peak country. I've got two kids, grown, or the same as. Lost my wife a couple years ago to ovarian cancer, which was a bitch and a half. Sucked the life and heart out of our kids, same as it did me. But it's like the tornado. Sometimes you can't outrun it, so you just try to knuckle down and get on the other side…"

Hank scraped a hand through his hair, then leaned back against the cement wall. "Anyway…technically I doubt I'm missing anything. I have to believe everyone at Griffin's doing the same thing we're doing here. Chipping in. Doing whatever they can to help everybody past the mess of this storm. I'll eventually get to my friend, but right now, it's no hardship or problem for me to be here. Just as soon be part of doing what needs to be done, getting everybody fed and sheltered and eventually put on their way again…"

Married, she thought. Not that that was a surprise. Everyone she knew—at their age—had been married at least once by now. Sometimes twice.

Still, she absorbed the picture of his life those few words had framed for her. He'd obviously deeply loved his wife. Loved his kids. Created a life that really mattered to him.

That long ago summer…that Beach Boy summer…he'd not only trailed after her like a lovesick puppy. He'd seemed sure of nothing he wanted from his life. He'd had no career goals, no life plans, hadn't been sure of a single thing. Except that he wanted her.

She'd wanted him, too. But that had been about hormones and desire, and her parents had drilled into her how much fun that was—but how irrelevant to real life. Even before high school, she'd had a mapped-out life plan, with the ambition and determination and discipline to follow through. And because Hank hadn't been on her schedule, she'd jettisoned her feelings for him like yesterday's newspaper—not without guilt or regret. But because that's what she thought she had to do.

And now…lately, it wasn't as if she'd changed her mind about what was right or wrong. It was just…

She wanted to be Peachy again.

She wanted, just once, to taste again what it had been like, to be young and high and so sure of everything. To be wanted more than anything else in life. At least in someone's life.

"Jane?" The pilot's voice interrupted her mental mulling. "Your turn. Where were you trying to go when we got hit with these tornadoes?"

Good question, she thought. And gulped down the last of the amber fire in her Dixie cup, only wishing the Scotch could enable her to know that answer.

"Well…I'm a lawyer. A contract lawyer. I made partner last year in the firm I've been with for the last nine years. I'm divorced. Three kids, one in Seattle, one in Alaska, and my daughter's still in college, but Angel's in Europe for the summer right now in a school program. My home base is in Connecticut, Branbury…."

Even in the dark, she could feel the others looking at her, waiting.

And abruptly she realized that she was willingly offering up the facts. The surface information that gave the impression of a successful, happy life. The surface information she always willingly offered to anyone who asked.

But the others had shared something more personal. More honest. More…vulnerable.

For the first time in a long time, she wanted to do the same. This back room was dark and quiet and hot. None of these people were ever likely to meet up with each other again. There was nothing to risk by offering something personal about herself out there.

But somehow…the words wouldn't come.

She tried to say something, but her throat dried up and she found herself swallowing, then swallowing again.

Finally she said, "Honestly, I haven't minded being here, helping out. So many people have it a lot worse."

She smiled, but it felt like a raw, fake smile. And when no one immediately responded or said anything, she lurched to her feet as if someone lit a fire beneath her fanny. "I loved the drink. Thanks for including me. But I just remembered that I promised to help one of the older passengers get settled…."

She barreled out of there so fast, she almost knocked over a waste basket. It took two fumbles for her to get the door open, but then she was outside, and the long, wide lobby of the terminal was darker than mud now that the sun was down.

A few yards away, two men were chatting, their silhouettes starkly clear against one window, the shadows of a husband and wife paired in another. The whole lobby had quieted down, with most trying to sleep. People had either grouped with newfound friends or whoever they'd been traveling with. Couples hadn't been separated, only the single passengers curtained off by gender. Jane suspected it wouldn't have mattered; the long, exhausting day had made almost everyone konk out early.

Not her. Her heart was beating louder than a noisy drum.

She wasn't used to acting like a fool. Not used to feeling like one. But the most unfamiliar sensation of all was tasting the flavor of loneliness, in her throat, in her heart. She seemed to be the only one wandering around solo.

Being alone was her own doing, her own fault, her own choice. She knew that. But the feeling of intense loneliness still burned, like the bullet of a sniper she'd never seen coming.

CHAPTER 4

When Hank pushed open the door, it was barely 4:00 a.m. The sun hadn't cracked the horizon yet, but the sky had softened to a dark pearl-gray. Clouds were still restless, as if they couldn't forget the tumultuous storms from the day before, but a few stars poked through the cover.

It was light enough to see—at least to make out vague shapes—but more important, it was fresh outside. Cool enough to breathe.

Airports were his bailiwick. Instinctively, his gaze took in the damage to ramps, service vehicles, gates, chevrons—all the things that were going to need work before the airport was fully functional again.

Only two planes were in sight. All the other aircraft had been moved safely undercover before the tornadoes hit. Fuel and cargo trucks also appeared to have been locked up tight before the storms. The control tower, he already knew because he'd spent hours there yesterday, was also in good shape.

The smell of soup wafted from their hodgepodge of an outside kitchen—the same steak soup they'd had for dinner and were probably going to have, in some variation, for the next couple meals as well. All freezers in the vicinity had lost power, and since steak was the most expensive thing being lost, it was the first food volunteered. Keeping the pots on the barbecue kept the food safe. Various passengers had volunteered to supervise the fire in shifts. The night volunteer was nodding off with a spoon in his hand.

The only other body outside was a small figure leaning against the outside wall.

Hank recognized her immediately, and hesitated—for a whole two seconds—before hiking over to her.

"Peachy." He spoke her name softly so he wouldn't startle her. She wasn't sleeping. Her tousled blond head was leaned back against the building, but her knees were cocked up, her posture clearly indicating someone who was tired but tense.

Her head whipped around the moment she heard his voice.

"Couldn't sleep inside?" he asked.

"I only wish," she said wryly. "But there's something about sleeping with a couple hundred strangers…."

He had to grin. "A little too personal for all of us, I'd guess." He edged down next to her, using the cool building for back support the way she did, cocking up his legs, same as her. Quietly he said, "Something seemed to upset you earlier."

She ducked that. "The whole group's great. So many people are pitching in to help."

"You, too."

"Yeah…but it's way easier for me to pitch in, than try to sit still with nothing to do." She added, "You seemed to get elected boss of this mess, whether you wanted the job or not."

"Actually, there's a formal hierarchy set up for crisis situations in public places like airports, but this…well, there just hasn't been a reason to nail down roles quite like that. Maybe they're giving me a figurative chair at the head of the table, but it's more politeness than anything else, probably because the two pilots have the rank of captain, where I'm a colonel."

She glanced at him, obviously not taken in by his self-deprecating tone. "So a colonel is way higher than a captain," she murmured.

Again he had to grin. She obviously didn't have a clue about military rankings. No reason she should have. And he'd had enough talking about the "business" of their situation. "Right now I'd about kill for a good cup of coffee."

She closed her eyes, obviously swept away by the same fantasy. "Hazelnut. No sugar, no cream. Just a fresh-brewed hazelnut…"

"Hell, don't do that. I can almost taste it."

It was her turn to chuckle, and Hank realized it was the first time he'd seen a spontaneous smile from her…and suddenly, there it was. Even in the predawn dimness, even in the disheveled shape they both were, even with all the years passed between them…he remembered that smile.

He remembered *her*, the way he hadn't before.

Their gazes connected, held. Suddenly the morning air was electric, the mist whispering around the dew-drenched grounds surrounding them in privacy. She was the only thing in life that seemed clear at that moment. Those amazing blue eyes. The petal soft skin, the thin little nose, the elegant cheekbones and high-arched brows. The tinyness of her. She was so short, so little, yet such a dynamo. A concentrated package of potent, pure female sexual energy.

He remembered that part of her as if it were yesterday. She'd always been so bursting with life. She'd always been driven to do things, to make a difference. She was passionate about every cause she took on, and had the backbone and determination to back up her dreams.

"Where *were* you going when we ran into that tornado weather yesterday?" he murmured.

"Right here."

"You mean *really* here? Kokomo, Indiana?" he asked disbelievingly.

She let out a humorous sigh. "Any way I say this, it's going to sound silly. Because it is. But yesterday morning, when I got on the plane...I was trying to follow an old summer dream."

"And that dream was...?"

"I wasn't headed to Kokomo, Indiana. I was trying to head for one of the Cayman Islands, the one that used to be named Kokomo. The one that was in the old Beach Boys song. Only a temp working in the office made the arrangements, and she apparently confused what I'd asked for and I was so darned busy I never looked or checked. She set up the tickets for the wrong Kokomo. It was just a totally silly goof."

He didn't know what to say. It *did* sound silly and impossible, but then, that was what mistakes usually were. Unlikely twists in the road. Stop signs no one noticed. "Okay...I remember the song. But...what does the song have to do with the old summer dream you were following? You mean...you always wanted to vacation on a Caribbean island?"

"No." The first peak of pink frosted the horizon. The light was suddenly perfect, but he could see her more clearly. See those startling blue eyes, the blush of color on her cheeks. "I meant...I got this idea...I mean..."

He sensed she wasn't used to stumbling over her words, that possibly he'd stumbled into touchy territory for her. But she was tired, and it was dawn, and they knew each other way back when. Maybe the circumstances encouraged her to keep talking, even if she found it hard.

"I had this idea," she repeated, "that I just once wanted to feel the way I had when I was seventeen. That summer of our senior year."

He turned his head, listening.

"I was a self-centered brat back then," she said wryly.

"Hey. No, you weren't."

"Yeah, I was. But the good part, the part I wanted to feel again, was just the flavor of being happy that way again. I was so sure of what was right and wrong, so sure of where I was going, so sure that I could have everything that was important if I just worked for it...I *know*, this all sounds ridiculous. It was ridiculous back then, too. Cripes, I can't explain this."

She was right. Nothing she said made much sense to him. But if the words didn't add up, her tone of her voice, her posture, her eyes did. She was unhappy. Terribly unhappy.

"You mentioned that you were a lawyer. A contract lawyer. If I remember right, that was exactly what you wanted, your law degree...."

"Oh, yeah. And that's just it. I bulldozed through life going after exactly what I wanted. And damn it, Hank, I *got* it. I was so positive that certain goals and achievements would make me happy. Instead, I feel as if I took a wrong turn. Back when

I was young. Maybe even back in that summer of our senior year...." She hesitated, turned to face him. A whispery breeze suddenly silked strands of hair across her chin. She lifted a hand to push them away, her gaze still on his, intent, electric. Out of the blue, she said, "You really don't remember me, do you?"

"Of course I do. We've both been talking about that high school summer, knowing each other—"

She shook her head, swiftly, fiercely. "Yeah. You remember me in some vague way. But not really. Darn it, Hank. I hurt you. I was a bitch times three. Selfish. Thoughtless. And since fate handed us this unexpected chance to see each other again...I just want to say I'm sorry."

Hank's first instinct was to say an easy, "Hey, it's okay, forget it," but it obviously wasn't okay for her, wasn't something she'd forgotten. He racked his memory bank for that long-ago senior summer.

He'd had an embarrassingly painful crush on her—but then, so had every guy in the senior class.

Jane was the class goddess.

He was just a guy.

She'd been passionately involved in everything—class politics, world causes, grades, music. She'd led the prom committee and the cheerleading squad and all that obvious stuff the girls tended to like, but she'd also been the kind to pitch in after a football game to help clean up—and to spur everybody else to help. She was zesty and fun, full of spirit and laughter. Everybody liked her, but the guys...well, the guys groveled.

She was a little tiny for the average goddess sex symbol, but her small size just made the guys feel more protective. She was blond and adorable and ultra-feminine right down to her fingertips. Her family had big money, but she never acted like it.

He'd taken her to the summer country club cotillion, but not because he'd ever expected it to happen. For him, it had been like a winning lottery ticket falling out of the sky. He'd never had any intention of attending the white-tux dance thing…until Peachy turned into his date.

It was complicated, the way social politics in an upscale suburb always were. Peachy didn't need a date so much as an escort. His father and her father were both on the planning board. They arranged it—not like medieval fathers forcing their kids into a marriage, but just manipulating their kids into being allied for this event. Why, Hank couldn't remember. If he knew at the time, he hadn't cared. He only cared about getting his arms around his goddess.

She'd paired up with him a few times before that, but no different than she'd done things with a lot of guys. She wasn't serious about anyone. If some event came up, she often impulsively included whatever guy was in her vicinity. God knew, he'd always made a point of being in her vicinity.

Hank remembered that dance. She'd come with him…but left with someone else.

He hadn't been exactly thrilled at that turn of events—but it hadn't hurt the way a bullet through his heart would have. At the time, it made sense to him. She'd gone off with a guy who was more in her league. Big money. Headed for an Ivy League college the way she was. When she'd taken off, there'd been no stunning blow, more like something he'd been waiting for—like knowing a final exam was coming, or facing a tetanus shot.

She was never going to end up with him, so he'd never allowed himself to fantasize in impossible directions like that. Hell, he was just glad to have the chance to do the escort thing, to get his arms around her for the dances, to have her looking up at him with those sassy blue eyes and perky grin.

"This is about that dance?" he asked slowly. "Your leaving with that other guy?"

She looked at him again. "That's part of what I'm sorry for, yes."

Now he felt even more confused. "There's more?"

"Yes. In fact, there's something I've been a whole lot more sorry for." And she reached for him.

If a lightning bolt hit him, Hank couldn't have been more stunned.

He was years distant from that green boy with his tongue hanging out from yearning…he'd been married, loved from the heart and soul, and of course he recognized the click of chemistry. But a kiss from her—he just never expected it.

They were on a tarmac in Kokomo, Indiana, for Pete's sake. The sun was coming up fast and bright now. Debris from the tornado dominated the view. Mosquitoes were rising, along with already choking heat, and the asphalt felt gruff against their butts. There was just nothing, anywhere in sight or sound, conducive to romantic feelings.

Neither was her kiss, for that matter. She just seemed to twist around on her knees—a totally awkward position for her—clutch her hands on his shoulders for balance and then, eyes closed, plunk her mouth on his.

It was a crooked kiss.

A silly kiss.

A downright embarrassing kiss.

Even so, he caught a whiff of something he remembered. A scent, a taste. The shape of her mouth, the tilt of her head. Something that stirred memories he hadn't even known were stored like treasure in the memory banks of his brain.

For a second or two, anyway. Because that was as long as the kiss lasted.

She reared back, still twisted on her knees, her eyes popping wide and looking straight into his.

"Damn it," she said.

"Yeah, that's what I was thinking."

"I'm sorry. Really sorry." She sank back on her heels then, but she was still facing him with a very odd, very determined, very thoughtful look.

He was looking at her, too, but not like before. He'd never felt fear flying an F-16, but her, now…he had the sudden, wary instinct that the bright, civilized, intelligent woman he'd once known as Peachy had a closet lioness in her. A lioness who could pounce without warning. "There's no reason to be *that* sorry," he said a little wryly. "I mean, I'm not sure what that was about, but…"

"I'll tell you," she said softly, bluntly. "I'd been thinking that there was a moment when my life took a major wrong turn, even if I didn't realize it at the time. And it was that summer you took me to that dance. The summer I took off on you. I remember the feeling when you kissed me, but the chemistry hadn't seemed that important then. I didn't value it. Didn't need it. Didn't think it mattered."

Whoa, he wanted to say, yet somehow couldn't. Between

no sleep, no breakfast, that ram of a kiss, and now her sharing fiercely private revelations…he just couldn't seem to process it all, not coherently. "Peachy," he said gently, wanting to stop her before she said anything else. Who knew if she might really regret sharing such serious stuff with a man who'd long become a stranger to her?

"That chemistry did matter then, Hank. But not now." She shook her head with a self-deprecating chuckle. "Well, maybe I'm *not* sorry I kissed you. At least now I know for sure it's completely gone. There's nothing there."

Nothing there?

Hank told himself the only reason he felt ripped raw was because she'd stabbed his ego. Okay, he admitted it, he'd wanted her to feel a mighty attraction to him. What guy wouldn't want the goddess of his teenage fantasies to feel uncontrollable desire for him? And that reason for his ripped-raw feeling was true. At least ten percent true. But the other ninety percent of his psyche was suffering for an entirely different reason.

Of course the darned woman hadn't felt anything. She'd jammed her mouth on his and lifted it two seconds later.

It wasn't just that her kiss had been pale.

A two-second smooch didn't risk a damn thing.

There was no good sex without risk.

And if she was that hot to dive into old memories, then so could he. Because the only gold to win in life happened when you risked it all.

So he grabbed *her* this time. But softly. Wrapped his arms around her shoulders this time. But slowly.

And he lowered his mouth on hers this time, but definitely not in a flat, aggressive smack. He took her mouth, one sip at a time, deepened the kiss, one taste at a time. You couldn't get down to the level of yearning, unless you opened your heart to it. He'd learned that...well, God knew when. He just knew it. The way anybody who'd had good sex knew it.

Didn't take long.

Not with her.

Her right hand had been in startled midair when *this* kiss started. Now it was clinging around his waist, kneading the skin through his shirt. Her spine had been stiff when he'd shifted her across his lap. Now it bowed, eased against his supportive arm. Her eyes had been stark open when he'd first hooked her close. Now those soft eyelids were closed, her pale lashes creating shadows on her cheeks, a flush of desire stroking her throat and cheeks with hectic color.

Oh, yeah. And she was kissing him back.

This was a kiss that involved tongues and teeth. A kiss that reached greedily for more feeling, more risk. A kiss that found both...then dove back for more.

Hank had the vague, mortifying awareness that he was turning back into an out-of-control teenage boy. He didn't get ruffled. In his life, in his career, control and character and strength were critical survival skills. In a crisis, he was the one who never lost it.

But he was sure as hell losing it now.

Again, suddenly, she jolted free, lifted her head and looked him straight in the eyes. Shock showed in her expression this time. Shock...and desire.

She started to say something, yet no sound came out of her mouth. Quicker than panic then, she pushed off his lap, stood, looked at the sun zooming up the sky, the light on the tarmac that hadn't been there minutes before, and shook her head as if she were trying to make sense from an incomprehensible world.

Again she tried to say something, but words refused to emerge from her mouth that time, too. Apparently giving up, she spun around, stumbled toward the door of the terminal, grappled twice with the pull bar before she could successfully open it, and then finally shot inside.

Hank stood and raked a hand through his hair. Nothing that just happened made sense. Nothing she'd done. Nothing he'd done.

He'd never been threatened by Peachy as a kid. Awed, yeah. Overwhelmed, oh, yeah. Wildly in-crush with, totally. But not intimidated by.

He couldn't think of much in life that intimidated him. God and war, naturally, but not people. People were mysteries he was interested in, comfortable with.

But the emotional place that woman had just taken him was an unknown, evocative ground, untested, off his map.

He was too damn old for those kinds of shenanigans, he told himself. But there it was. His heart was thudding like a muffled engine.

The man fifty yards across the tarmac—the volunteer manning the massive soup pots—had woken up and was standing up now. He waved, and if Hank wasn't mistaken, winked.

Pretty obvious he'd seen that kiss.

Pretty obvious he'd thought Hank had something hot going on.

Hell. The tornado was beginning to look like a lot easier crisis than Jane.

CHAPTER 5

Jane tottered back into the terminal lobby and was immediately assaulted by the heat and rush of smells. It was the second day of no air-conditioning, no showers, and intrepid heat and humidity. The repercussions were starting to add up.

The smells weren't unpleasant—yet. But it'd be a good thing if they could air the place out today…better yet if they could all start leaving before much more time passed. And the chaos took her mind off Hank, at least for a time.

The night before, she'd set up a spot to sleep near the door. Now she dug in her bag, found fresh clothes and some toiletries and started trying to do a shape-up. She had makeup wipes to freshen her face. Deodorant. Under a light blanket, she peeled off clothes, pulled on yellow shorts and a wild yellow print top—one of the few outfits she'd tossed in for the island.

She ran a brush through her hair, pushed bare feet into flip-flops, and searched through her bag in the dim light until she finally located the finger-size teeth cleaners she always carried on planes.

By then, three people had yanked on the blanket to talk to her.

Because she was still rattled over Hank, the errant thought

slipped into her mind that it would be impossible to have a love affair here. Even a one-night stand. Even a quickie. There wasn't an ounce of privacy to be had for love or money.

Not that she was thinking about quickies.

"What, Delores?" As she zipped up her bag, she found the new-age lady with the flowing gray hair, wringing her hands again.

"Someone took my celestite this time. I tried to find you before. But once everybody started getting up and moving around this morning, it was all crowded and confusing. And that's when I think somebody got into my suitcase and stole the celestite."

"Darn," Jane murmured.

"This isn't like the hiddenite. I *have* to have the celestite. It came from my grandmother, you see. It only works if it's given by a relative, so it's not like the thief could get any benefit from it. And it doesn't work unless the person's connected to both Capricorn and Gemini."

"Which of course you are," Jane said.

"Of course—"

"Have you been outside for breakfast yet?"

"I couldn't eat. I've been too upset."

"Okay. I want to hear all about the theft, but first let's go by your things, get any medication you're taking, then head outside for a little nourishment."

"I—"

"I know. You couldn't possibly eat. But you can tell me more while we're walking, okay?"

That idea calmed the older woman almost immediately. "Celestite works on the throat chakra, but that's not the point.

The point is that it helps one get one's equilibrium back. It helps calm a person. It's been *very* hard to be calm since the tornadoes—"

"Yes, it sure is. That celestite—it's kind of a blue-white stone, isn't it?"

"Actually, it's a mineral, dear. Not just a stone. And this one has the darker blue shade, so it's much more powerful."

"And the points always have to point toward the sky or it doesn't work," Jane said, earning a huge sigh of relief from her ethereal sidekick.

"I knew you'd understand. So many people treat me like a batty old woman."

"No," Jane said disbelievingly, gave the older woman a hug, and moved on to the next problem.

People were increasingly anxious to contact loved ones, to get answers about when the airport would be running again, about how, when, and where they were getting out of here. There was plenty of food, because the loss of electricity meant everything in any freezer had to be used up or risk being spoiled, so there was still no end of stuff to fill the big pots outside. But they were going to run out of dishes or paper ways of serving things before much longer, and clean silverware was worth gold.

"You know…" A man named Ralph was helping her move a chair, using it to prop open a door to let more fresh air into the lobby. "I can't say I'm glad this happened. But…it's all kind of interesting. I never thought about any of these problems before."

"Neither had I," Jane admitted.

"Anything else we need to move?"

"No, but…you know where we've got all those people camped on the floor by the west entrance? I don't suppose you could coax them to relocate a little so there'd be a clear path to the door? Last night, people complained they couldn't move without stepping on someone else. If we could help them organize a little better…"

"Done," Ralph said, and took off.

A man broke his glasses. A rubber band provided a makeshift fix, but it took a while to locate a rubber band. Someone else needed first aid cream for a blister. The captain was organizing groups to move debris off the tarmac, so Jane put out the word. Another small group was walking outside, hoping to assess the vicinity around the airport, to see if there might be transportation or power within a walkable distance—or, for that matter, if there were others who needed help.

Jane kept thinking that she wasn't doing enough. She didn't know anything about sanitation or electricity or communications or any of the serious things going on. Yet by the time she ambled outside to grab some lunch around two, the bright hot sun illuminated two scrapes on her hands and a healthy bruise blooming on her knee.

"What on earth did you do to yourself?"

Hank's voice shivered on her nerves like a brush of silk. She whirled around. It was the first time she'd seen him since early that morning. She'd told herself that she'd forgotten that exotic embrace between them—or imagined its power—but seeing him invoked fresh nerves all over again.

"I haven't a clue," she answered him, glancing down at the scrapes and bruises. "I haven't done a darn thing—"

"That's not what I've been hearing. The crew says you're the one keeping the passengers from imploding."

"Honestly, that's not true. Almost everyone's pulling their weight and then some."

"That's what I see, too. A few complainers, but that'd be true in every situation. And people are worried and frustrated. Who wouldn't be?"

He was holding a bowl, so was she. Almost everyone else had eaten lunch by that time. There were no surprises in the menu, beyond a few more peas and corn in the steak soup.

"I have to admit, I'd sure like a few more choices," she murmured.

Hank swiped two bottles of warm soda. "We're fast getting out of the mainstream drinks, too. Clearly mango guava juice was a little over-ordered by concession lady."

"I think most people are still thinking of it as picnicking, though. Making do."

"Me, too. But as soon as this is over, I want a drink with ice. And nothing that looks like hot soup."

"You're not kidding. Especially the ice!" He was making it easy to be with him, as if that wild moment that morning had never happened. That was okay by her. Nothing wrong with denial when a girl was desperate. She sank down in the shade of the building next to him. Since that morning, she was amazed how much had been done. "The whole tarmac looks cleared. I can't believe it!"

Hank nodded. "I don't know how soon we'll get repairs

done from yesterday, but planes should start being able to land again shortly. And a truck made it from the Air Force base this morning—"

She was listening, but when he lifted a spoon to his mouth, she saw the streak of blood on the back of his arm. "Hank, what did you do?!"

He glanced down. "I think my elbow had an argument with a pair of pliers. And the pliers won."

"That needs some serious first aid, if not stitches."

"Says the lady with her own set of cuts and scrapes. And the blister on your hand has to smart."

With some bemusement, she noticed the bubble on her right palm. It looked particularly startling against…well, against such a pampered hand. She'd always had a major female streak about manicures, nice hand creams, pretty nails. Or she had until two days ago. Oddly enough, she felt a weird pride in the blister. "You know, it didn't hurt until you brought it up."

"That's it, blame me for your working like a dog," Hank teased.

She grinned—but then devoured the completely boring and unappetizing soup. For someone who loved sushi and a raw shrimp salad for lunch, preferably served with sterling and a snowy white linen napkin, she seemed to be falling on the soup like a pig—and a greedy, hungry pig at that. "You're getting some first aid cream and a bandage for that arm, mister, just as soon as we finish lunch."

"And you're getting first aid and bandages for some blisters, missy, so don't try arguing with me."

"I suppose we could have an argument about who's bossier."

"I suppose you'd win," he said wryly.

"Of course I'd win. I'm the woman."

She yanked his chain for another few minutes, effortlessly, easily…before it suddenly hit her that she'd turned back into a teenager. Just like that, she was flirting with Hank again. Teasing a boy. Shooting him smiles and insults.

On top of an embrace that was still frying her brain when she thought about it.

Which, of course, she wasn't.

"Wait a minute. You said an Air Force truck made it here this morning?" By then they'd dumped their dishes and she was steering him toward the terminal office that stashed the first aid supplies.

"Yeah. We've been trying to pass the word. There probably isn't going to be electricity for a few more days yet. The whole town and surrounding area was hit by tornados, so there's no end of repairs that need to be done. But emergency services are now up and moving."

Two of the passengers were nurses, who'd been manning the first aid supplies since yesterday. But no one was there when Jane poked her head in, and it wasn't like it took a brain surgeon to clean his open cut and use some antiseptic.

"*Hey.*"

"I'm sorry. There's no choice. Without plain old soap and water and sanitary conditions not exactly on a par with the Ritz afraid you really need an extra shot of alcohol there. In fact, I think you need a tetanus shot—"

"No."

She chuckled. "There isn't one. Relax. But how'd you get to be a colonel and still be such a sissy?"

"It's easy."

"Come on. Suck it up. The worst is over. Now it's just some antibiotic and a good tight bandage. I really think you should have a few stitches, but hopefully if the tape is snug enough, the cut will seal okay." Fixing the cut was no big deal, yet she still felt intensely conscious of his skin, the warmth of him, the closeness. She kept waiting for a sense of responsibility and guilt to hit. It didn't. Instead, she just kept wading in that tickle of desire whisking through her. How long had it been since she'd felt that basic old hormonal rush? It was fierce. Fun.

Silly.

But welcomed.

Suddenly his eyes were meeting hers again. "You were real brave when you were holding the alcohol, cookie. But now it's my turn. Let's see that blister."

"Hey," she yelped.

"Now how did you get to be a cutthroat, high-falutin' heartless lawyer if you were still such a sissy?"

"It was easy."

"Come on," he said. "Suck it up. It sounds like we're both going to be here for a maximum of another twenty-four hours."

"Pardon?" The sudden change in conversation shot her head up. He'd been holding her hand. Treating her blister with some kind of balm. That's all she'd been thinking about, all she'd been feeling, but now…she had to listen.

"We're definitely on a priority list to get us all out of here. Air Force base will make that easier. The National Guard's priority yesterday was taking on the sick and vulnerable, but we're not far down on the list after that. Kokomo doesn't need more visitors to feed and house. They'll get us shuttled out of here by late tomorrow, onto flights leaving from Indianapolis. You can pass the word along. I'm guessing it'll perk everyone up."

"Yeah, it will," she said. But it was weird, how low her heart suddenly sank.

It was going to be over. Soon. No more sleeping with a bunch of noisy, snoring, coughing strangers. No more bad smells. No more steak soup. No more dark, no more inconveniences, no more incessant heat. Life would get back to normal, with fresh showers and clean hair and real food. Computers. Cars. The whole ball of wax.

"Everyone'll be thrilled," she said hollowly. And tried to grapple with why she felt suddenly as if someone had socked her in the teeth. It was just…she'd been busier than a one-armed bandit. She was busy in her regular life, of course. Beyond belief busy. But here, she'd been feeling…useful. Feeling good. Feeling, well, young again.

"Peachy?" She felt Hank's knuckles gently touch her chin, coax her face up to his. "Hey." His tone lowered to baritone-butter. "What's wrong? Are those tears?"

She looked up at him. And then couldn't. A thug of emotion seemed to slug her in the heart. It hurt. The way her heart hadn't hurt in a very long time. She should be wanting to go back to her wonderful life. But the truth was…she didn't. Something was right here, that hadn't been right in her life in a very long time.

"Peachy?" he said again.

"I'm fine," she said. "Just had something in my eye." What else could she say? If she tried to really explain, he'd think she was crazy. Hell and a half, she knew she was reacting crazily. She didn't suddenly think Hank could or would or should be part of her life again. It was just…those kisses. And that for the first time in years, she'd felt young again. Young and bursting with hormones, bursting with hope and life. Feeling zingy and zesty on the inside. Feeling female. Inside and out.

"Okay, just say it. Whatever's wrong—"

But obviously she couldn't. And since she seemed stuck being in an immature, foolish way, she did what any mom knew worked. She took an immediate time out. Jerked to her feet and got out of Hank's sight.

Once away from the privacy of that back office, back in the wildly busy terminal again, her pulse almost immediately calmed down. People aimed for her faster than bullets—two had complaints, two had an argument they wanted her to settle. A man recovering from surgery had lost his walking cane. One of the passengers had seemed to disappear; no one knew where she was. And there was that announcement to spread through the group—that rescue was on the way and they'd be out of here as soon as sometime tomorrow.

She'd always loved it. Trouble. Confusion. The stuff normal people ran from. Probably she'd been drawn to lawyering because she loved sorting out messes, prioritizing the right from the more right, the wrong from the most wrong.

But right now, it wasn't about that. She just wanted to be too busy to think, and that was easier to accomplish than breathing. Every minute involved dealing with the unpredictable and unexpected and sometimes zany, working with all these strangers that she'd somehow bonded with.

Halfway through the afternoon, one of the airport staff tracked her down. She'd been outside, bringing a tray of drinks to the wheelchair group playing cards in the shade. "Got a message for you," the man named Brian told her.

She cocked her head.

"Your kids. Bry? Lar and Angel? They all knew the flight you were on, knew from the news that your flight had gotten stranded, didn't want to clog up emergency channels to find you…but they were worried. So they went through the National Guard to make sure you were okay. The message was that they loved you and to get in touch when you get out of here."

She smiled. "I've got great kids."

"Sounds like it."

She calmed down another notch. Hearing from the kids always did that. Even though they were all pretty independent now, launched in their own lives, the connection reminded her that wonderful love was just as real, even if they were physically distant from each other. It wasn't as if *everything* was wrong with her life.

It was just that *something* was.

And it had taken a tornado to make her notice.

Late afternoon, a big, noisy camouflage truck barreled down the runway—bringing everyone out of wherever they'd been hanging out and creating the atmosphere of a party. The guys had been delivering supplies to a local hospital and clinic. They had no news other than what the group already knew— that roads were being cleared, and they could expect buses to pick them up by late afternoon the next day to head for the Indianapolis airport. But they also brought supplies—boxes of ice and water, and enough plastic dishes and ware to get them through another day.

It wasn't as if they'd been stranded for years, but Jane found herself as boisterously happy as everyone else. The new bodies bought news. A reason to laugh. Stories to share. Affirmation that they'd all be home soon, that others were all right, that the tornadoes had destroyed tons of property but there'd been no deaths, no serious injuries.

Twice, Jane found herself searching the crowd for Hank.

The funny thing was...he was easy to find. He was everywhere, and since he was a half head taller than the average man, he was also easy to spot. And every time she located him, she found Hank looking straight at her. Finding *her*.

Unfortunately, there always seemed to be a dozen bodies between them. Or she'd be in the middle of a conversation or something else that had to be finished, and by the time she freed up to approach him, he was out of sight again.

Hank often seemed to be coming in and out of the air traffic control area, or hiking toward the plane maintenance area, or with the crew of people moving debris from the tarmac and roads.

Those were natural places for him to be, just like it was more natural for her to be in or around the terminal, because that was where the core group of passengers gathered—especially those who weren't as able and tended to have special needs.

By dusk that evening, though, the truck was long gone, dinner was long over, and Jane found herself outside. A group of passengers had congregated there and were just absently shooting some bull. Jane kept thinking what a motley and unlikely group they were—an old man with fierce eyebrows, one of the teenagers, a married couple who'd been headed to see their grandchildren, a nerdy kid from a prep school who'd been coming home for the weekend.

They all looked like fellow ruffians, with dirty hair and wrinkled clothes in general. They'd all snuck outside because of the heat, because they had nothing better to do. And normally they'd have nothing in common, but that was the thing.

They had the tornado in common.

They been stranded and survived and had each other in common.

Carl, the white-haired man, was a local farmer and looked the part. "Can't believe I'm stranded ten miles from home all this time. And when I get home, Leah's going to hose me down before she lets me in the house...." He shook his head, making them all laugh.

"I feel like I've been a year away from the Internet and e-mail." Rob, the studious young man, leaned his head back. "Last week, I couldn't have imagined it. But it hasn't been that bad."

"I don't think so, either," Margie, one of the volunteer cooks, piped up. "Something happens like this, it really shocks you into thinking, doesn't it? Nothing in life looks the same."

"We'll all be glad to get home after this," Carl said.

One by one, they wandered away. Rob wanted a walk. Heather wanted to find her friend. The others were hoping to settle down for the night, catch some sleep.

She wanted to do the same, yet she didn't go in after the others. She leaned back against the cool wall, closing her eyes, realizing yet again how everyone else couldn't wait to get home—except for her.

It wasn't that she didn't want to go home. She loved her home. Loved her kids. Once upon a time, she'd even loved her job, her whole life. Everything she worked for.

But she still didn't have a handle on what had gone wrong. Why and how she'd become a bitch. Why all the things she'd wanted so much, once upon a time, now seemed to give her no sense of satisfaction or reward.

"Peachy?"

Her head jerked up at the sound of Hank's voice.

CHAPTER 6

Seeing Jane, all alone, her head bent in a posture of such dejection…made something snap inside Hank.

She'd been on his mind all day. The way she'd suddenly taken off after he'd bandaged her hand. The hot sparkle of tears in her eyes, not because of the blister, but because of something else. Something that tore at his heart, just from looking at her face.

And that wasn't even counting the Armageddon of kisses from before that.

She lifted her eyes when she heard his voice. Dusk was falling fast now, the violet sky dusting everything with a soft jeweled glow. The same artist's palette colored her face. Her skin was so soft against the silhouette of the cement siding; her eyes, so full of shine and emotion.

"You're not sleepy yet?" he asked her.

"I only wish."

"Come on. Let's walk then."

"All right. Where to?"

He steered her toward the far hangar. Planes were his turf.

And almost everyone was settled down in the terminal or around the main buildings.

The minute they ambled inside, it was quieter. Cooler. A pair of guys were smoking, leaning against the outside wall, but when they saw him and Jane approaching, they waved and wandered off.

Deeper inside, it was darker than pitch, but an LED pocket flashlight illuminated the open door of a plane. The interior had been in the process of being cleaned when the storm came up, because the door was still open, a vacuum still in the aisle, trash scooped up and knotted tight. It was just empty. Port windows gleamed like black mirrors.

He clipped the LED light to the window. The light didn't reach the corners, but at least relieved the darkness. "Just sit anywhere," he suggested.

Instead of taking an airline seat, she eased down to the carpet near the open door and galley, near the glow of that pale light. He poked around, emerged with two mini bottles. "Scotch, I think. Pretty hard to see for sure. For darn sure, there's nothing to dilute it with."

She chuckled. "It'll do."

He decided to talk to her about his sons. Just because he'd wanted to tell her something more about his life. "They're both terrific kids. Bruce lost his way for a while, flunked out of college—but since then he's hit his stride, back to school, good job, the whole thing. Just got in with the wrong girl at the wrong time. Then the right girl at the right time. He's one of those men, where the woman in his life is always going to make the whole difference. He's never good when he's alone, needs the home thing. It's not how young men think. They're supposed to think of themselves as being happy and carefree when they're bachelors. But he's my nester. Makes money hand over fist now, a baby on the way."

"You like your daughter-in-law?"

"Adore her. She was there for me, when my wife died. Just as much as my sons were."

By then he'd long hunkered down next to her. Both of them had kind of leaned back, half lying, looking either at each other or at the glimpse of stars from the open doorway. For a moment, though, a silence fell between them. Her eyes honed on his in the dark. And like she knew what he was thinking about—maybe what was hovering in her mind, too—started talking again.

"How about the other son?"

"Johnny." He gave a wry sigh. "Handsome as hell. Broken two hearts that I know of. Short of smacking him upside the head, not sure what I can do. He falls in love, then gallops down the road when it comes to commitment time."

"How old?"

"Twenty-four."

"Young yet, Hank."

"Yeah, I know. I wouldn't even want him settled yet, but I still worry about the pattern. He finished school, spent six months bumming in Europe on a shoestring, came home broke, thought he'd loaf around the house. And I let him…I *know* I should have gotten tough, but the truth was…I liked having him around."

"Is he still living with you?"

"Nope. Finally got a job. Boulder, Colorado. *Not* an adult job, mind you, but at least there's a faint glimmer of responsibility showing up."

"And you're in Colorado Springs, so you can see him."

"Yup."

"What was she like, Hank? Your wife?"

He checked her mini bottle, but she was sipping it mighty slow, was a long way from a refill yet. So was he, but the subject made him pause and take a swallow. "She was...sturdy. Not in looks so much, as on the inside. Physically, she had kind of dark blond hair, always a sunburned nose. You'd never catch her inside if she had any excuse to be outdoors. She was raised an army brat, the kind of woman who..." He hesitated again, trying to frame his words. "She was the kind of woman who stood next to you. Not a lot of talk, but never running away when the going got tough."

"You loved her."

"With all my heart," he freely admitted.

"Anyone since?"

He said, "I want there to be. Some people don't understand that—how you could look for someone else if you lost a mate you really loved. But that's just the point. I know what a good marriage is. I know what good love can be. I'd want it for her. I want it again for myself."

"Of course you do."

"It's not that easy to find."

"No."

Her small laugh was as intimate as a kiss, making him think he'd better start another conversation, fast. "Your turn to spill. What was your ex like?"

"Hmm. Cray was good-looking. Smart. Came from a great family. He was...charming. An active dad, always happy to be with the kids, play with them."

"Sounds like a paragon. Only there has to be a catch or you'd still be married."

"Yup. He worked the first three years we were married. Then I got into a seriously good law firm, started bringing in real money. And he quit his job and started spending it. At first, that was totally okay with me. We both wanted a parent home when the kids were young. But then…it wasn't about parenting. He was always out playing, not there for the kids. Took up one expensive hobby after another. Spent days at the country club, just hanging around. He was an active, involved dad. Still is, in fact."

"But…"

"But he stopped pretending he was ever going to look for work. He liked his life, just as it was. Maybe that shouldn't have mattered to me." She looked up, an honest question in her eyes, one that had clearly haunted her. "I mean, what difference does it make if both have a formal job? Especially if one is more than capable of bringing in an adequate income for the household. It bugged me that I was being sexist, thinking the guy should pull some financial weight…"

"Maybe I'm reading something into this. But it doesn't sound as if the problem was about money."

She nodded, releasing an old sigh. "You said it. Money was the symptom. Not the illness itself. Cray…he liked playing for a lifestyle, had no interest in changing. And I stuck it out for a lot of years because the kids were happy enough. It's not as if we were fighting and they were exposed to a lot of anger. But…at some point, it finally hit me, that he wanted my paycheck more than he wanted me. There hadn't been a real marriage in a long time."

"You didn't see it?"

"I hadn't wanted to see it." Again, she looked uncomfortable, as if she didn't often talk about her marriage, herself this way. Yet she didn't seem unwilling, only awkward at trying to get the words out. "I wanted to think that the man I was married to…loved me. Corny, huh? But that was the part that…shamed me. Diminished me. It's hard to explain, but when someone just stops loving you, not for a *reason*, but just because the feeling dies….I felt as if I were invisible. Not worth the emotion. Not important enough, interesting enough, to stir any emotion. I felt like a piece of furniture, a thing…."

Hank reached for her.

He didn't know how or why he'd started this conversation. Talking about exes and divorces and failed marriages sure as hell wasn't his thing. For that matter, he wasn't dead sure why he'd coaxed her into this walk, initiated the contact to begin with.

But he knew exactly why he reached for her. Knew exactly why he hooked an arm around her shoulder and leveled a long, hot kiss on her mouth.

Life beat everybody up. Nobody was exempt. Everybody lost the full-of-hell arrogance they had in their youth.

But he hated it, that Peachy had been beaten down. Yeah, she'd been thoughtless as a kid. But she also put out five hundred percent of herself, all the time, to everyone, to everything. She left a lot of dust in her wake because she moved so fast. But nobody should have used her like that jerk had. Nobody should have taken advantage of that big heart, that exuberant energy, that hope and zest that had been so much a part of her.

That someone had cruelly taken her for granted killed him.

That someone made her feel like less of a woman killed him more.

That was his excuse for the first kiss. And the next five. And then, what the hell, he stopped pretending he needed excuses anyway.

"Hey," she murmured a little later. By then her yellow print top was gone. So was his shirt. One of her sandals. His shoes. "Are we really doing the swept-away thing? At our age?"

"I don't know what *you're* doing. But what I'm doing is living out an old summer fantasy. I used to daydream that you were crazy about me, couldn't get enough, were so hot to sleep with me that you couldn't stand it." He lifted his head from the delectable taste of her shoulder for a solid five seconds. "What can I say? I was a seventeen-year-old boy. Seventeen-year-old boys are always the star in their own fantasies. It's not my fault."

She chuckled…and then willfully arched her spine to invoke more full body contact between them. It was the kind of invitation he'd dreamed of when he was seventeen.

Come to think of it, he still dreamed about stuff like that.

But he'd also always dreamed about being a good lover for his woman, too. Then and now.

For damn sure, he wasn't leaving Peachy with any doubt about being wanted. About how special, how sexy, how unforgettable, how totally un-invisible she was.

The utilitarian airline carpet was a long way from a luxurious mattress. There were no pillows and the aisle was as narrow as a twin bed. Even with the open door, it was almost airless inside. Yet the physical discomforts of their surroundings only seemed to work for them, or so Hank thought. The miniature LED light hardly illuminated the deep darkness—not a night this dark, this hot.

But the heat that mattered was coming from her, not the temperature. And the intense darkness magnified his sensory awareness of her—her silky hair, drifting though his fingers. The satin smoothness of her skin, damp, sweet. The sound of her—not the sounds of an untried girl, but the sounds of a woman who wanted to be loved.

Peachy knew what she wanted, knew what she felt. Knew exactly how much trouble two adults could get into, if they really really worked at it.

And he was sure willing to work at it.

"Hank?" she murmured a while later. Two orgasms later, to be precise.

"Hmm?" Right then, he admitted conversation was the last thing on his mind...until she asked him her next question.

"Why did I ever, ever let you go?"

"Beats me. I was the best crush you ever had."

"Why didn't you tell me that at the time? Why didn't you chase me harder?"

"You're making this my fault?"

"That we never had sex before tonight? Damn straight. How could it be my fault? I had no way to know how good you were."

He had to grin. And tuck an errant strand around her ear, just so. "Hey, Peachy."

"What?"

"You were the fabulous lover, not me. In fact, you were

beautiful, fabulous, and breathtaking. Better than any fantasy I ever had. And believe me, seventeen-year-old boys can have some Pulitzer prize level fantasies."

Initially she fell silent. "All right. I can't top that as a compliment. Or I *can*…but not until I catch my breath."

He didn't want her to catch her breath.

He wasn't dead sure he was up for a second round, hadn't tested the capacity of his virility in quite a while—and he kept hearing from guys his age that second and third rounds had gotten tricky. But maybe they were wrong.

Or maybe Peachy just inspired him to extraordinary heights. Or maybe depths.

"That was a sick, sick pun," she whispered later.

"I'm just saying. Who knew at my advanced age? So it must be your fault."

"What's *your* fault is that I'm probably going to walk bow-legged for quite a while. With rug burns on my fanny and whisker burns on my throat."

"And elsewhere."

She laughed, low and soft. "And elsewhere, you wicked man."

JANE WAS PRETTY SURE they dozed once or twice—at least she did—but every time she opened her eyes, they seemed to be talking. Not about anything heavy or meaningful.

He described his house in Colorado Springs.

She described her Connecticut place.

He told her about flying F-16s.

She told him about making partner and getting the kick-ass front office.

He talked about how lonely he'd been after his wife died, how dating sucked—but coming home to silence sucked even worse. He admitted how for a long time he just couldn't sleep in the king-sized bed without a body next to him. And he admitted, for a while, that he'd tried drinking himself to sleep, so he wouldn't have to face that lonely insomnia.

She told him how angry she'd been after the divorce. About how she hadn't wanted to be with anyone. How she hated being set up. How she hated sleeping in a king-sized bed alone. How she'd tried drinking herself to sleep with wine, but that hadn't worked, so she'd bought a queen-sized bed and gussied it up with fabulous 800 thread count sheets and down comforters and lace-edged pillows.

"Did that work?"

"Of course not. Nothing works," she said wryly. "Thank God time eventually makes it easier."

"For me, too. I don't mind being alone some of the time."

"Neither do I. I was lonelier in my marriage than I was after. There are parts of being single that I really like."

"There are parts I like, too. Like…eating what I want. When I want. Not having to clean up anyone's messes but my own."

"No one to say 'I'm sorry' to."

She hesitated, not wanting to disagree with him, but she had to add, "I know it sounds goofy, but…to be honest, I miss having a body to say 'I'm sorry' to."

He hesitated then. "Hell. So do I."

When dawn was breaking, when she walked back to the terminal with him and separated just inside the door, Jane had the craziest, funniest realization. She was happy. Exhausted to beat the band, but still, exhilarated, smiling-on-the-inside happy, kicky-high. Soft happy. Honest happy.

Yet when she walked inside the women's room and clicked the latch on the stall door, she felt the sudden shock of huge, fat tears welling in her eyes. Welling, and then stinging out of control.

She sank against the door. That first round of tears turned into an inexplicable flood. She didn't even know why she was crying, but it was as if someone had flipped open a faucet and there was no shut-off valve.

Nothing seemed to stop it. She couldn't seem to catch her breath or her control.

For Pete's sake, she really *was* happy. She didn't regret a minute of the night with Hank—not a minute, not a second. She'd desperately wanted that chance again—the chance to feel the way she had that summer when she was seventeen, when all things were possible, and she owned her life and herself, and the future spread out in front of her with a limitless, wide-screen horizon.

Maybe that was what the tears were about. Rediscovering, through making love with Hank…

All she'd found.

And all she'd lost.

CHAPTER 7

"Jane! Jane! Are you in here?"

A trio of excited female voices made her gulp fast. Two seconds later, the women were pounding on the stall doors. "Are you in there? Jane, we need you. They said the buses are coming early! We're getting out of here! But Mary Bartholomew lost her glasses. And one of the men fell on a piece of glass. And—"

"I'm coming, I'm coming." Well, she wasn't coming *quite* that fast. Cripes, she hadn't even had time to pee, much less finish up her own personal meltdown. At least there was so little light in the restroom that no one could likely tell her eyes were red-rimmed or her hands were shaky.

And after that, there was no time to worry about herself anyway. The terminal lobby was in complete chaos. Actually, it had been in complete chaos for the last two days, but now it had turned into a regular Armageddon.

People had spread out their belongings over the whole lobby during the last couple days. Now they were trying to gather it all up. Immediately.

To add insult to injury, it had started raining—not a friendly little soaker but a heat-breaking torrential downpour. The gloomy skies made the terminal darker and frayed tempers. The group who'd done such a great job of being good to each other and coming together suddenly seemed intent on having a group nervous breakdown.

"But Jane. How is Wilbur going to know where I am? What if no one picks me up?"

"But I don't understand, Jane. I don't think my flight leaves out of Indianapolis. I don't know anybody in Indianapolis."

"Jane! The captain told me that Henry and Bud are going to be on the first bus, and not me. I think I should be on the first bus. I have a bad knee—"

"Jane! Someone took my blue jacket!"

"Jane! I can't close my suitcase!"

"Jane! I can't find my suitcase!"

The co-pilot found her sometime before noon, shook his head when he found her knee-deep in the middle of some strange man's shorts and socks. "Is it like this for you at home?" he asked her wryly. "Every time I turn around, you're getting stuck with doing something you shouldn't have to do."

"Everybody's pitched in where they could, don't you think?"

"Not like you have. And that's why I stopped. Just to say…I'm sorry we met during a tornado, but hell, I really am glad to have known you."

Startled at the praise, she gave him a warm hug—but then went back to it. Through the whole chaotic morning, Hank still dominated her mind. Last night clung to her consciousness like dew on morning grass—and so did trying to understand the inexplicable crying jag she'd had earlier. It all seemed mixed up with the whole crazy scene. Here she was, two days dirty, her hair unmentionable, no makeup, wearing clothes meant for some dad fool resort that she was probably never going to actually visit.

Yet above it all, beyond it all, she felt a sense of pride in herself that she hadn't felt in years. All the real accomplishments, all the stuff she'd achieved and worked so darn hard for and fought to win...yet here she was, separating two seniors from bickering over socks, and she felt proud of herself?

Maybe the tornado had brought on a heretofore unrecognized lunatic side of herself. Who knew?

Who had time to find out?

When the first bus left with a load of passengers, she looked around frantically for Hank. Everyone wasn't leaving at the same time, but she had to find him, had to speak to him before the chance was gone.

She'd already told the captain that she wasn't on the fast track many of the other passengers were. Of course, she was hot to get out of here, just like everyone else—but she had a week's vacation, and most certainly wasn't going near any Kokomo island at this point, so for her, it was just a matter of getting home to Connecticut. Others with more pressing responsibilities or problems could go first.

Only it didn't work out that way. For her or for Hank. Once the buses got there, they were herded like lemmings, no way to slow up the whole process.

Bare minutes before noon, Hank suddenly showed up in front of her, a bag in his hand. "Peachy, you're harder to find than a raindrop in a storm."

This was so *not* how she wanted to say goodbye. She knew

she looked like hell and a half, and there was just no way she could say anything meaningful, anything personal, with a zillion people milling around them—even assuming her tongue wasn't suddenly drier than the Sahara, which it most definitely was.

Still. She was an adult, not a seventeen-year-old girl any more. So she listened, while he explained there was a car waiting for him, and he was stuck on a fast exodus out of there. Then she straightened his collar, and took a good memory-installing look at that handsome face and roguish smile.

"If you think I'm going to forget this tornado, you're crazy," she said.

"If you think I'll ever forget *you* again, you're even crazier." He bent down, bussed her cheek—then hooked his jacket over his arm and leveled a serious kiss on her mouth. Not a long kiss, but one that was deep and hard and real.

She caught her breath. Or tried to. "If you'd kissed like that when we were seventeen, I'd never have let you go," she scolded.

"If you'd let me kiss you like that when we were seventeen, your dad would have gone after me with a shotgun."

"My dad was a pacifist."

Hank shook his head. "No dad is a pacifist where his gorgeous teenage daughter is concerned."

She knew people were looking at them. So did he. His vehicle was waiting for him; the driver had already honked twice. They could hardly hold everybody up so they could keep on flirting like a pair of immature teenagers.

Yet he touched her hand once more, and looked at her

once more—not like teenagers, not like flirting—but as if he really cared, as if she'd really touched him.

God knew, the last two days with him had really touched her.

And then he was gone. Striding away. Out the door…and out of her life.

WHEN JANE STEPPED OUT of the Lexus, the wind whipped open her suit jacket. It was the last day of summer. She could smell it in the wild, warm wind, in the brush of leaves in the air.

She raced up the steps to the lobby of Bentham, James, Lambrect and Whitcomb and escaped inside. Her three-inch heels clicked down the hall toward her office, sounding like a fast tap dance. A two-point-five million-dollar deal had gone down at lunch today, maybe not the moon, but still a big enough kerchunk to make her day when she nailed it. So maybe the three-inch heels and kick-ass Elie Tahari suit weren't factors, and possibly—the day after she was dead—she'd stop being quite so superstitious.

Interns scurried past her. A couple of the partners hung by the water cooler. She gave them a thumbs-up as she soared into her office—and then her ebullient mood suffered a tiny tank. Her office didn't look exactly like a pigsty, but it was getting there. The weeks since her return from Kokomo had been jam-packed with business. Pyramids of files jockeyed for space on her desk. Pink and yellow slips decorated the surface by the phone.

Marcia—the temp who'd turned into a full-time girl Friday as of three weeks ago—showed up in the doorway, looking wary and ready to run if need be.

"How'd it go?" she asked carefully.

Jane bent down, rooted in her purse, and emerged with a bottle of Pinot Noir—San Ventre, 1997.

"Oh my God, oh my God," Marcia said. "For me?"

"And some extra loot in your check this week. We both put in a lot of hours on this nightmare. Appreciate all you did."

"You already gave me a raise—"

"Yeah, well, this is just some extra loot because you've had to put up with me. Who else would?" Jane grinned as she motioned toward all the notes. "Any calls that won't wait?"

"Two of your kids called. They were afraid they wouldn't catch you tomorrow for your birthday. They both said they'd try you later."

"They will. Or I'll call them, so it's on my dollar." She slipped off her suit jacket, then kicked off her heels and plunked onto her office chair. "My daughter's coming home from Europe on Friday. I'll be gone from the office as of noon."

"I'll bet you can't wait to see her."

"I can't. Best birthday present I could have." Without thinking, she started humming an old song. The title escaped her. It was just one of those really, really old ones with a catchy tune, the kind that you couldn't let in your head because you could never get it out again. They'd been playing it on the radio on the route in from the restaurant. "Aruba…Jamaica…um, Marcia, this call from Griff Johnson. Was he ticked off again?"

Marcia's face changed expression. Her posture went from smiling and relaxed to smiling and just a wee bit wary again. "Truthfully, I've never spoken to the man when he wasn't ticked off. He wanted some further information on some tax ramifications—"

Jane nodded. "It's all right. That's what I thought. Every time he calls, he seems to think someone here should just instantly have an answer for him that second. Next time, put him straight to me. You don't have to put up with that verbal abuse from anyone, Marcia. Don't think it's expected. It'll never be expected. But we're almost done with this contract issue for him, and then that's the last we have to see of him."

"Thanks." Marcia suddenly shook her head with a little laugh. "Where's my boss?"

"Pardon?" More of those lyrics kept echoing in her head. Come on pretty mama…

"The bitch," Marcia said gently. "We're all wondering where she went. What you did with her. If she's ever coming back. Where you buried the body."

Jane laughed…but moments later, after Marcia left and she was digging through the archaeological mounds of work on her desk…it hit her. She was still humming.

Her inner bitch really was gone.

So was all that anger.

Nothing had been the same since the tornado…since that god-awful campout and steak soup in Kokomo.

Since Hank.

Friday afternoon, she drove to the airport to pick up Angel. Her youngest daughter walked off the plane, looking like a train wreck—blond hair all tumbled, sleepy eyes, clothes all wrinkled. Jane took one look and, laughing, wrapped her up in a bone-snuggling hug. The others had left the nest, and this one was about to. The summer in Europe had clearly matured her yet another notch, but even this exhausted, her baby looked precious and young as grass. "Happy to be home?"

"I had a *great* time. The whole summer was beyond copacetic. But yeah, I can't wait to have my own bed, my own pillow. I'm starving, Mom—"

"I expected you would be." It had to be fast food on the way home—specifically French fries—because Angel claimed she'd die if she couldn't have them immediately. She talked nonstop about what she'd seen, what she'd done, how she could hardly wait to get back to school, how she was sick of school, how her brothers were, how she'd gotten food poisoning in Venice, how she'd fallen in love in Vienna, how it had been dying hot in Rome...

They were just walking in the door, dragging heaps of luggage, when Jane's cell phone sang. She clicked the on button, even as she started turning on lights through the hall and living room.

It was only when she recognized Hank's voice that she stopped buzzing around. Actually, everything seemed to stop. Her feet, her hands, her brain. Her heart.

She was so stunned to hear that melt-quiet baritone that he spoke again. "Peachy? This is Peachy?"

"Yes." She shook her head and laughed. "Yes, of course it is. I just didn't expect to hear your voice. I didn't think you knew where I lived. I mean, we didn't give each other phone numbers or addresses...and I just didn't think that...I mean, you live so far. So I..."

Angel backed up from the kitchen to the hallway stairway to stare at her. You'd think she'd never heard her mother stutter before. Or maybe she'd never seen her mother sink down on the third stair step, a phone to her ear, and flush the color of rose petals.

When the call was over, Angel was still studying her as if a prehistoric archaeological artifact had suddenly been unearthed in her home. "What," she said, "has been going on while I was in Europe?"

"Nothing, honey. At least…I didn't think anything that momentous was."

"So who's the guy?"

"Who said it was a guy?"

"Mother." In two syllables, Angel expressed a symphonic range of dry humor. And then she looked hard at Jane again. "My God. You look younger. Did you have a face-lift?"

"No, of course not!"

Angel approached and squinted at her hard now. "And you look…oh my God. Happy. Not tired or stressed. This is getting scary. You either tell me who this guy is or I'm calling my brothers. Where does he live? How serious is he? How serious are you? When am I going to meet him? What's he do for a living? Mom, you're not sleeping with him, are you?"

Jane stood up, hooked an arm around her daughter's neck in a mini-stranglehold, and dragged her nosy, prying youngest into the kitchen. She might just answer some of those questions. Later. When she was ready.

Just then, though, she just wanted to bask in that private, summer-warm feeling for just a few moments longer.

It wasn't Hank who'd changed her life. It was her. But he'd enabled her to remember what she'd lost, what she'd been missing.

Because of him, she'd taken a risk she'd been afraid to take for a very long time. To open up. To love.

To be loved.

He was flying this way in three weeks. Angel would be back in school by then. Jane would have the house to herself. She'd agreed to see him.

She wasn't going to put a fancy word on her hopes this soon. But now she knew—those old summer dreams hadn't died... but only opened up the possibilities.

* * * * *

Be sure to return to NEXT in August for more entertaining women's fiction about the next passion in a woman's life. For a sneak preview of Miriam Auerbach's DIRTY HARRIET RIDES AGAIN, coming to NEXT in August please turn the page.

CHAPTER 1

As weddings go, it was a little…unorthodox. And that was before the body turned up. But I'm still getting ahead of myself.

Let me begin by stating immediately and emphatically that it wasn't *my* wedding. Please, that's not gonna happen (again). At thirty-nine, I've been happily widowed for four years since shooting my abusive husband in self-defense. That act of freedom really made my day and earned me the nickname Dirty Harriet.

My real name is Harriet Horowitz. The wedding in reference was that of my best buds, Chuck and Enrique. Now, seeing as these are two members of the male persuasion, some people would say it wasn't a real wedding. To them I would say, "Get a life!"

Chuck and Enrique's love was true and just, which is why I was there that April Sunday, standing up for them as Best Human in their commitment ceremony. I was standing, to be precise, at the altar of the Church of the Gender-Free God, waiting for the groom to walk down the aisle.

In honor of the occasion, I had ditched my daily uniform of black leggings, black tank top, riding boots and leathers when I dismounted my trusty steed—my 2003 hundredth-anniversary Harley Hugger. I wore a floor-length silver gown, matched by four-inch sandals and shoulder-length silver earrings. I'd had my normally wild dark hair blown out, and it hung down my back in long silky perfection. My green eyes were fully lined and mascaraed, and my normally bare, raw nails were painted Princess Pearl.

The proceeding seemed to be taking its sweet time, though. Outside, I heard the unmistakable potato-potato-potato rumble of Harleys. Ahh…the day's musical entertainment had arrived, in the form of the Holy Rollers Motorcycle Club and Gospel Choir, a group of five black drag queens whom I had met at the rehearsal dinner the previous evening.

I knew they rode their Hogs in full riding gear, so it would take them a while to change into their wigs, makeup, bras, girdles, gowns and all. So I would be standing here in my misery a while longer. I tried to take a deep breath to send some healing oxygen to my aching back and feet, but my chest wouldn't expand beyond the rigid steel cage of the corset. I coughed and staggered, drawing all eyes to me. Great. As if I really wanted to be the center of attention here. Apparently my cough provided some kind of permission to the assembly to engage in similar behavior, as there followed a flurry of throat clearing, foot shuffling, seat adjusting and other expressions of discomfiture.

Finally the nuptial procession started with the entrance of the Holy Rollers.

As the happy couple reached the altar, the Rollers, with perfect timing, ended in glorious harmony, "Free at last, free at last. Thanks God Almighty, we are free at last."

Yes! Thanks God Almighty I would be free at last of this

sartorial straitjacket, not to mention the grinding organ noise. Just as soon as the Reverend Botay arrived, the vows would be exchanged, the blessing bestowed and we'd all be outta there and off to the reception at Hog Heaven.

So, okay…where was she? Minutes passed as we all looked nervously at each other. Okay, I know I said all weddings have snags, but enough was enough. I'm an investigator, after all. With a "Don't worry, I'll take care of this" nod to a baffled-looking Chuck and Enrique, I set off to investigate.

I headed past the altar, where a door led to the back rooms. The door to the reverend's office was half-open. Just as I was about to rap on the door, I saw the poor woman crumpled behind her desk, her violet-and-white vestments flowing about her petite body. Rushing over, I could see clear as day her skull had been smashed in, and her black hair was matted together with blood. The murder weapon was lying right next to her, also covered with blood. A big metal organ pipe. No wonder that monstrosity was emanating those bloodcurdling screeches.

Bile came up my throat. I ran into the adjoining bathroom and dry-heaved in the toilet. I couldn't believe it. The last two weddings I'd attended had both ended in tragedy. Maybe marriage really was a dangerous proposition. Yeah, okay, so I'd been the perp last time, blowing away my husband at a friend's wedding reception. But how could this be happening to me again?

Then my conscience, always a little slow on the uptake, came online. What the hell was I doing feeling sorry for myself? A good woman, a woman of peace, had been savagely slain.

It was time to act. I pulled out my cell and called the cops. Dirty Harriet was on the case.

REQUEST YOUR FREE BOOKS!

2 FREE NOVELS PLUS 2 FREE GIFTS!

Next™

There's the life you planned. And there's what comes next.

NEXT07R

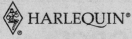

COMING NEXT MONTH

#89 WHOSE NUMBER IS UP, ANYWAY? •
Stevi Mittman
While redoing the local bowling alley, decorator
Teddi Bayer finds murder on the scorecard—members of the
bowling league are being knocked off like pins in a strike
after all chipping in to buy a winning lottery ticket. Soon
the killer targets Teddi—and detective Drew Scoones seems
too distracted by Teddi's charms to come to her rescue!

#90 DIRTY HARRIET RIDES AGAIN •
Miriam Auerbach
Harley-riding P.I. Harriet Horowitz thinks she's seen it all—
until an unusual exchange of vows gets even stranger when
the reverend turns up as a corpse before the first
"I do." There's a twisted killer on the loose in Boca, and
it's up to Harriet—with the help of stud muffin sports
trainer Lior Ben Yehuda and her pet alligator, Lana—to
crack the case.